I0714474

Also By Joe Moore

The Santa Claus Trilogy

Believe Again, The North Pole Chronicles
Faith, Hope & Reindeer
Glaciers Melt & Mountains Smoke

Return of the Birds

Santa's Famous, Incredible, Flying Reindeer

Santa's Elf Series

Santa's World, Introducing Santa's Elf Series
Jamie Hardrock, Chief Mining Elf
Shelley Wrapitup, Master Design Elf
Keeney Eagleye, Naughty/Nice List Manager
Sara Buttons, Master Doll Maker
Ford MacHarley, Master Wheelsmith

The Faces of Krampus

By Joe Moore

and

Illustrated by Mary Moore

Published by The North Pole Press

Published by The North Pole Press

Smoky Mountains, Tennessee
ISBN13: 978-0-9992977-0-4

Cover design by Mary Moore

Copyright © 2017 by Joe Moore

Library of Congress Catalog # 2017951758

This is a work of fiction. Names, characters, places and incidents are either the product of the author's imagination or are used fictitiously, and any resemblance to actual persons living or dead, companies and business establishments, events or locales is entirely coincidental or used in a fictitious manner.

Information about and for this book may be obtained through contacting North Pole Press at: Info@thenorthpolepress.com.

Printed in the United States of America

DEDICATION

This book would not have come together if a good friend of mine hadn't placed it squarely into my head. I find it amusing how a simple joke turned into something special for me. It was when Jordan Keene said to me joking around "I have the heart of Krampus".

Now Jordan stands seven feet tall and would give a bear pause. But this man is as gentle as a kitten, and has a huge kind heart to match his enormous frame.

I answered his remark saying, "Then Krampus has a very gentle heart!" And that is how it began. So, this book, which had the working title of 'The Heart of Krampus', is dedicated to the giant with the gentle heart, my good friend, Jordan. Thanks, Bird.

ACKNOWLEDGMENTS

It is difficult to write in a vacuum. Obviously, the writer knows what is going on with the story and they can explain things if you ask. However, without the aid of the writer standing right next to the reader, things can get lost in the translation. In other words, the reader doesn't know what the heck is going on in the writer's mind.

Enter my editor, Gary Brown. Because of his efforts, it is almost a guarantee that you will not only be able to follow my thoughts, but you will enjoy this book infinitely more than its rough draft version. Gary made numerous suggestions (in addition to all my grammatical blunders) that helped this writer (me) explain the actions better to the reader (you). My sincerest thanks for a job well done, and I look forward to our next collaboration.

In addition to Gary, as always this book would not exist without my lovely and talented wife, Mary Moore. She not only did all the illustrations that you will see in this book, but she designed the cover, formatted the book, added all the paraphernalia, and made it quite enjoyable for me to write it. She is my muse and inspiration and is always encouraging me to write my heart and my stories. This will actually be my 11th book, and Mary is behind each and every one of them. Thank you, my dearest love.

My last thank you goes out to you, my readers. Over the years I have received countless wonderful comments and whether it's my children's series written by me and illustrated by Mary, my Santa Claus Trilogy, or even my reign of terror book Return of the Birds, the compliments and encouragements I get from you, my readers, help spur me to continue writing and bringing you stories.

This is the fourth genre that I have ventured into. And while it is written as a Young Adult book, I hope that all ages will enjoy this. It loosely ties in with the Santa Claus Trilogy but is meant to explain a completely different part of the Christmas holiday season. The thoughts and history of Black Peter and Krampus are generally tied to traditions and events in Europe, but I have added my own twist and tied several characters together into one being. I hope you enjoy reading this book as much as I enjoyed writing it.

INTRODUCTION BY SINTERKLASS

Krampus is a demonic monster. He has large sharp horns that curl like a goat's. He carries a horrible stench, has a long sharp tongue, cloven hooves for feet, a full coat of coarse black fur, evil red eyes, and nasty, razor sharp claws. This half-goat, half-demon arrives on December 5th, the eve of the Feast of St. Nicholas with ill intent. He carries a basket of switches — long willow branches he uses to beat children who have misbehaved.

But far worse, he takes children to his underworld, where he keeps them there. They become his slaves and are beaten and tortured constantly until they can be trusted to behave properly.

Krampus' name is derived from the German word krampen, meaning claw. He is said to be the son of Hel in Norse mythology. Hel, the daughter of Loki, is the goddess over the dominion known as Hell. Krampus, shares characteristics with other scary, demonic creatures in Greek mythology, including satyrs and fauns.

The legend is part of a centuries-old Christmas tradition in several countries even today, where Christmas celebrations begin in early December with the Feast of St. Nicholas on December 6. Krampus was created as a counterpart to the kindly St. Nicholas, who rewards children with sweets or treats in their shoes or boots that have been left outside for his visit. Krampus, in contrast, would swat "wicked" children and steal them away to his lair.

He has done this for centuries. And since this terrible demon arises only in December, the chance of seeing a child that was taken is nonexistent until the following December — if ever.

The legend of this half-demon, half-goat is only partly

true. Actually, the Krampus that this book is about refers to my father's friend and companion. Who was my father? He is known by many names: Viejo Pascuero, Julemanden, Joulupukki, Weihnachtsmann, Babbo Natalie, Pere Noel, Mikulas, and Sinterklaas to name a few. You most likely know him as Santa Claus. I am his son, and I took over my father's job in 1954, and I am the current Santa Claus.

But, the story about the real Krampus started long before he came to be with us in the North Pole. It is about as far from his legend as anyone would believe.

CHAPTER ONE

His true name is Petrus Schwarztale, which is German for Peter Black.

Peter's parents were not particularly attractive. In fact, the word ugly was used on more than one occasion when describing them. So when they had a child in 1752, that baby was exceptionally difficult to look at. As he grew, Peter's looks did not improve much. He had a pointed nose that curled down almost like a bird's beak. His chin came to a sharp point and this poor boy's ears not only came to a point but were so large they flopped over under their own weight.

His eyes were extremely dark, and it was difficult to distinguish any color in them beyond black. His large heavy brow always appeared to be scowling because his forehead couldn't prevent it. He had moles on his chin and forehead that would not be called beauty marks. Finally, he was much smaller than anyone else his age. His parents knew Peter would be lucky to reach five feet as an adult.

When he was able to attend the school he was continuously ridiculed and picked on. He wasn't even through his first full week when it happened.

"Hey ugly," a boy a few years older and quite a bit larger than Peter yelled to him.

Peter ignored the boy and kept walking.

"You, you hideous looking troll!" the boy continued, "Why don't you crawl back under the rock you came from?"

"Leave me alone. I am not doing anything to you," Peter said.

"Not true. Your ugliness is hurting my eyes!" At this, the other kids began to chortle. This seemed to spur the bully more and he walked up and shoved Peter to the ground.

Peter stood up and brushed himself off, saying nothing.

"Why bother cleaning yourself off? I think the dirt goes better with your ugly face," the boy said and pushed him down again, this time into a mud puddle.

As his clothes were now soaked, Peter debated as to whether he should get up, or just stay on the wet ground to see if the boy would go away. As he was thinking this, the boy started moving toward Peter with fists clenched. Just as he started to pull his arm back, the schoolmaster began ringing the bell for class. The boy hesitated for a moment and then lowered his arm.

"You better not let me catch you after school. I will beat the ugliness right outta you!" the boy said loudly so everyone could hear. He then turned and moved toward the sound of the bell.

Peter pulled himself out of the puddle and tried his best to clean himself up. He moved to the door of the school and the headmaster pulled him aside and yelled at Peter, "What is the meaning of this? You look like a pig! How dare you come to my school looking like this. You are a disgrace."

Peter tried to interject what had happened, but the schoolmaster wouldn't let him speak. The other children just giggled as Peter was admonished.

"You go home and don't show up here again until you are presentable. I do not allow pigs in my classroom." He turned from Peter, herded the other children into the classroom quickly and closed the door.

Peter stood staring at the closed door for a moment and then returned home. When he told his mother what had taken place, she said she would have a word with the schoolmaster.

Peter looked horrified. "Please do not do that! I could tell in his eyes he did not want me there. He was not interested what happened, he just wanted me gone."

His mother said, "Oh, Peter, you do not know that! He was probably in a hurry to get his class started. You are too hard on yourself."

But deep down she suspected Peter might be right. She thought she might wait and see if this happened again before going to the schoolhouse.

The very next day was a repeat of what happened, adding a bloody nose to the event, he was told by the headmaster to go home and not return.

He said to Peter, "You are too much of a distraction for the other children. How can I be expected to try and teach them if they are focusing their attention on you?"

The year was 1761. Education was not as advanced, although Peter now at age nine still desired to read, write and learn the basics of mathematics and science. He cried the rest of that day and well into the next. That was when Peter's father decided to teach him his profession.

"It's something you can do and have scarcely any exchange with other people," said his father, Karl. Karl Schwarztale was a master chimney sweep and ever busy with many customers. Being a solitary man himself, he always enjoyed his profession and took tremendous pride in it. He thought this would be an ideal career for his misshapen son.

As softly as he could, he told Peter, "I will teach you what I know about reading and writing, though I am not very advanced with my own knowledge on these subjects. I, too, did not go to school and most of what I know I learned on my own."

So the following day Peter joined his father's side as an apprentice and began to learn the craft of chimney sweeping. While it was less common in Germany for sweeps to use helpers in their craft, it had become customary in England and most of the work was done by "climbing boys" who could fit through the increasingly narrow chimneys. Around the time of Karl's apprenticeship to become a master sweep, it was learned that the more narrow a chimney, the better the draft.

Karl was a good size man just under six feet and about fourteen stones, so he had difficulty in the newer chimneys, which were only fourteen inches by nine inches. Many of the larger homes also had chimneys that were angled, or joined to other flues, making the task more difficult.

By comparison, Peter was small, shy of four feet. He was rather skinny, as well. The latter came partially from the fact that although Karl was always in demand, being a chimney sweep did not pay well. It was considered work that was demeaning to the vast majority. More often than not, he was able to bring just enough food home to keep his family fed.

He and his wife had always wanted another child, but it was beyond Karl's meager capabilities to support a larger family. While they would admit that Peter was no joy to gaze at, he was always a good, kindhearted boy, who did as he was told. So Karl dressed him in the traditional black garb of a chimney sweep and took Peter to his first client of the day.

As they walked to the house, Karl started teaching Peter about the various brushes and what each was good for. He explained how a chimney worked and how, depending on what was burned in the firebox, he would find different types of soot and ash in each. He warned his son of the dangers of rotting chimneys and to beware of loose bricks and stones that could come crashing down on him.

Karl knew the dangers of his occupation and was aware of the reckless abandon that master sweeps treated their apprentices in other countries. While not common in his country, most of the sweeps in other parts of Europe used indentured young boys and girls as slaves. Mostly they provided them with a corner to sleep and just enough food and water to do their bidding. Many were badly burned, cut, and far too many died from uncaring masters unconcerned for their minimal welfare. Some might think Karl was throwing stones at a glass house, but he knew he would treat his son as best as he could given their circumstances.

The conditions of a chimney sweep were harsh and the work was hard. Children that were used as climbing boys were often scared to climb into the narrow passageways. He'd heard stories of masters lighting fires as they worked in the flue. This was to get them to climb higher or work faster. Thus coining the phrase "to light a fire under you".

But he also knew that with the help of his son, he could increase the number of clients he could take care of in a day. Karl was getting older and already had respiratory concerns that were inherent from the result of years of soot and carcinogens that belched forth from the black surfaces that he cleaned and scraped. He felt a twinge of guilt thinking how he was condemning his son to a similar fate. But he could not see a higher destiny for Peter. Besides, more patrons meant more coin and a better lifestyle for them all.

As they approached their first client, Karl said to Peter, "Pull your hat lower over your face. I do not wish to have the owner see how young you are." Actually, he did not want the owner to see how repulsive his son was either, but wouldn't hurt his feelings saying as much.

The owner paid no attention to the boy behind Karl and merely led him to the first of several chimneys needing to be cleaned. Karl laid out several sheets on the floor to keep the soot and ash from spreading elsewhere in the room. He was grateful that the chimney had not been recently used so it was cool inside the flue. He knew that if it had been winter that probably wouldn't be the case.

He laid out several brushes and showed Peter which brushes to use, where, and how best to use them.

"Okay, son, now strip down to your underwear and get climbing."

"What?" asked Peter. "Why do I need to get undressed?"

"It will be a great deal easier for going through angles and corners for you." Karl said, "I am familiar with this house and the chimneys all have sharp corners that you will otherwise get caught on. Be careful not to cut yourself on them, either."

Peter did what he was told and grabbed two of the brushes. He went into the firebox and up the flue. His father told him he would take care of the base of the chimney and the first eight or nine feet as Peter did the rest.

"What you need to do is push your back against the chimney and tuck your knees and elbows in front of you. This way you can climb up the flue and brush as you go."

At first, Peter had trouble maneuvering through the chimney but he soon began to get the hang of it. As Peter moved into the darkness he realized he began to feel a calmness he had not felt in a very long time. Darkness enclosed him like a shroud. The cool surfaces felt good on his naked skin. As he scrubbed the ash and dirt away from the surface he gagged and choked on the abrasive material. He taught himself to take deep lungfuls of air and then brush the soot while holding his breath. Once the material abated, he released his breath blowing the dust away from him.

After some practice, he was able to hold his breath for a goodly amount of time. He shimmied higher and came to the first angle in the chimney. He easily navigated the change and worked on his back to clean the upper part of the flue. Because there was no place for the residue to go but onto him, he had to hold his breath longer until he could maneuver back onto his stomach and shake the sediment off his body.

He could feel his head beginning to pound and his desire to take a large breath fighting his every movement. At last, he finished the section and as quickly as the cramped space would allow, he turned over and shook and brushed the grit off his small torso. He swept the debris into the lower chimney and watched it float down toward his father.

Luckily for Karl, he had finished most of the lower portion and was away from the base when all the dirt and ash fell into the firebox. Not having an apprentice before, Karl never thought about having to beware of falling refuse from above him. He made a mental note that he would have to be vigilant, lest he get pelted by his son's work.

"How's it going up there?" he called up to Peter.

"I am almost to the top," answered the boy.

Karl was impressed with the speed of Peter's work, assuming he had done all that he should. But Karl wasn't concerned. He knew how meticulous Peter was about most things, and had little concern that the opening was now as clean as it would ever be swept.

When Peter reached the top of the chimney he yelled down a question. "Papa, should I just start at the top of the next one and work my way down?"

Karl barely caught the question through the muffled bricks. He thought for a moment and yelled back as best he could. "Yes, go ahead." He then coughed out a load of black phlegm.

Peter moved to the next chimney on the roof and began

his descent. He found it much easier sweeping the ash ahead of him then coming up from underneath. Again, though he could barely see after several feet, he felt a relaxed calm working in the dark. He wondered to himself if his eyesight would improve with time in this shadowy new world he was exploring. He would ask his father if his did, later.

Karl followed the manor's proprietor to the next chimney. He could already see traces of his new apprentice's work coming through the opening. He hurriedly opened the sheets to catch any more of the debris before it got on anything in the room. He had no sooner gotten the first two sheets opened when a large plume of ash fell through the opening. He decided he would have to wait until his son was finished before he would stick his head in there.

Karl knew he would have to rethink his whole approach to his learned vocation now that Peter was on the scene.

At their next appointment, Peter hit his first challenge, as the chimney had fallen into disrepair and some of the bricks were beginning to rot and crumble. His father came in from the opposite side of his son and showed him how to reconstruct the damaged area. Peter watched as his father deftly reassembled the broken opening and sealed the damage.

"You will need to teach me how to do that," his son said with admiration.

"I will, gladly. Now let's get the rest of this chimney cleaned."

By the end of their ten-hour day, they had done eight different clients. This was the most Karl had ever accomplished in a single day. His pockets were practically bulging from the proceeds. He now understood why other countries used helpers so regularly. He also wasn't nearly as dog-tired as he normally would be after a long day like this.

Peter was exhausted, but he knew he had accomplished a great deal and felt good over the effort. He was pleased with his father's excitement over the day's proceeds. Only one customer had made a reference to Peter's looks.

He said, "Wow, this one looks like he has fallen a few times already." Once the man learned he was Karl's son, he made no further mention of the boy.

When they got home, Karl spoke with pride about how Peter was a natural at this work to his wife, Hilda. He also showed her the amount of money they were able to make and her already large eyes bulged more.

Over the next several years the father and son team worked well together. Karl was able to increase his number of clients and the family fared much better than when Karl had done this alone. But each year Peter noticed that his father coughed more frequently, and often more violently. Some of his coughing spells would last up to a full minute. Karl also had trouble breathing occasionally, and the two would have to stop on their way to the next client until Karl could catch his breath.

One day Peter was in a chimney almost to the opening when he heard the proprietor call up to him. "Hey you, you'd better come down here and quick! There is something wrong with Karl."

When Peter reached his father, he was crumpled on the floor near the firebox. "Papa!" Peter cried. Karl looked at him with watery eyes and was wheezing mightily. He couldn't respond to Peter and just looked solemnly at his son and then closed his eyes.

Peter told the owner he would return tomorrow to finish the job and clean up. The owner agreed and growled, "See that you do." In truth, he wanted the man gone before he died, and he was left with his hideous son.

Peter covered his father up in one of the unused sheets and put him in the cart that they always used to move around the items needed for their jobs. As Peter strained to push the cart, which was near twice his size with his father in it, he watched his father strain to breathe as he came in and out of consciousness.

When he got home he helped his mother get Karl into bed. Once settled, he ran off to get a doctor. The doctor almost did not come at first, and Peter had to give him money up front in order to do so.

The prognosis was not good. Too many years of ash and soot had taken its toll. Karl couldn't breathe well enough to keep his organs functioning with oxygenated blood. By the time Peter had returned the next day from cleaning the rest of the previous owner's chimneys, his father had died.

Hilda and Peter buried Karl two days later. There were only a few other people in attendance. Karl was liked, but not well known, and only one client showed to say goodbye and give Peter and his mother his condolences.

Peter told his mother he would keep the family business going and that although they would miss his father dearly, she had no cause to be worried. That was a grossly optimistic of the events that were about to take place.

CHAPTER TWO

There was no question that Peter had become an accomplished chimney sweep. Over the last few years with his father, Peter was doing nearly all the work, including any repairs, and had rebuilt a couple chimneys for clients who had let them go so long that a fire had destroyed their old fireplace. Karl was the face of the team, and though certainly not a handsome one, his was preferred by far to the craggy and marred face of Peter.

As Peter went around to their old clients, at least half of them said his services weren't needed, and the rest offered to let him do the job at a fraction of what they paid Karl. While totally unfair, Peter would take the job to get something rather than return to his mother empty-handed.

What made the days worse was now that he wasn't accompanied by his much taller father, many children would ridicule him. Often they would come up as he pushed the heavy cart and swat him with birch branches or throw rocks at him.

Several times he had to stop pushing the cart to take refuge behind it, until the jackanapes ran out of projectiles to throw, or just gave up. He began carrying sticks and branches of his own to thwart their attacks. It was happening more often as if the word had spread through the village of the easy mark he was.

The larger problem was a few of the adults sided with the children and often laughed at their cruelty toward Peter. More often, parents were rarely around to dissuade the children from their torment of the hapless sweep. Some parents would stop the kids from persecuting Peter and occasionally would swat the children for their misbehaving and cruelty. The others would herd the kids back into the house without a word.

Towards the end of the year without Karl, the times became nearly insurmountable for the Schwarztale family. Peter had difficulty making enough money to exist. His clothes were now frayed and tattered, and the more disheveled he became, the less business he was able to secure.

Food became little more than the bread Hilda was able to bake and some water. His mother never complained once and always just smiled and said they would get by, and "better days were ahead". Peter was less optimistic, and most days he had difficulty raising himself from his cot.

As winter descended, they scarcely had enough wood to keep their fireplace lit. Occasionally, Peter would wrap a couple log pieces with the discarded ash and bring it back to the shack. He would sleep curled into a little ball with only a threadbare blanket to keep him from freezing to death.

That Christmas Eve there was a knock at their door. Peter was home as the days were short and his effort for the business that day was nearly fruitless. So it was a welcome sight when he opened the door to one of his father's old clients.

"How can I help you?" Peter asked the man.

"My chimney seems to be clogged and I can't get a fire going."

"Well, I have finished for the day, and it is Christmas Eve." Peter decided to play hardball as this was one of the people who unceremoniously turned Peter away the times he asked to service them again.

"Yes, I know." The man fidgeted with his hat. "Look, I'll pay you twice your normal rate if you come fix it tonight. I have asked other sweeps and none will come."

TWICE! Peter thought. He might actually be able to get some food for Christmas after all. He stayed calm and said to the man, "Well, if it is that important, I suppose I can see what is causing the problem. Let me get my tools and I will accompany you back."

The man cringed at the idea of walking back to his manor with this creature. He said, "You know where I live since you have been there before. I have another errand to run, and I am in a hurry, so I will meet you back there. Go ahead and get your things and I'll be waiting for you."

"Very well, I won't be too long." Peter closed the door and sighed. This would go a long way to providing for them.

It was beginning to snow as Peter pushed the cart along the road. As he was making his way to his destination one of the older kids came out of a house. He saw Peter and yelled out, "Hey look! It's the troll again!" He picked up a stick from the wood pile and made his way over to Peter who was trying to pick up the pace.

"I told you before, we hate trolls!" the kid yelled and swung the stick so hard it broke on Peter's back.

"Owww!" Peter cried out. He grabbed one of his tools and was about to swing it at the youth when he heard a voice from the house the child came out of.

"Don't you think about it!" A man was standing in the shadow of the front door. "Hans get away from him. Get in here right now."

Hans retreated and Peter was about to say something but thought better of it. He started pushing the cart again. His back stung from where the boy struck him. Another welt, he thought and pushed onward.

By the time he got to the house and knocked on the door, it was quite late. The man opened it and ushered Peter to the main living area and its stopped-up chimney. Peter could smell the smoke emanating from the firebox before he reached the room.

"I will need some water to put that fire out before I climb in there."

The owner just nodded and went to fetch the water.

Peter began laying out the sheets and loosening the strap that held his brushes together. He guessed that the smoke duct had not been cleaned since he was last here with his father, but didn't ask the proprietor when he returned. He just doused the fire and went to work after the smoke cleared a bit.

He pulled out two of his heavier brushes and began working around the base. He could tell immediately that his suspicions were correct based on the amount of creosote where the stack narrowed. He worked his way further into the opening and began climbing up the flue, working the excess slag and dust on the interior as he went.

A few more feet in he found the obstruction. The smoking remnants had built up so much that there was barely a passage through. Peter was amazed that the soot didn't catch fire and burn the house down. He needed to use the handle of the broom to punch the largest pieces clear of the stack. As he lunged another thrust and heard, "Hey! Be careful with that thing. You could hurt someone!"

Peter nearly fell out of the vent with shock and surprise. He quickly made his way down the chimney and came out of the firebox just ahead of another figure that was all dressed in red and holding a big bag.

"What are you doing here?" Peter asked when he looked at the man.

"Unless I'm mistaken, it is Christmas Eve, is it not?" The man answered.

"It is," stated Peter.

"Then I am doing my job delivering presents. The bigger question is what are you doing here on Christmas Eve?" The big man chuckled as he asked the last part.

"I am doing mine. We needed money for food, so I took this job," Peter said.

"I am surprised to see an elf down here. Let alone an elf cleaning chimneys."

Peter rose to his full four feet seven inches and said, "I'll have you know I am an accomplished master chimney sweep! And just who are you calling 'elf'?"

"Um, you. What is your name anyway? Mine is Sinterklass"

"My name is Peter Schwarztale."

"All right Black Peter, I have a question for you. I have some food in my sleigh that I would like to offer you and your mother if you'd allow me to help."

"How did you know I live with my mother?"

"Call it a lucky guess, I have to leave some things here. Why don't you clean and pack up here and we shall leave together? I have a couple stops on our way but I will bring you and your equipment home."

"I have my cart and tools with me. And tell me, if you are the real Santa Claus and you know where I live, how come you never came by before?" asked Peter.

"The more important issue is that I am here now. Let's just go with that, shall we? I can get everything in my sleigh. Now I am on a tight schedule, so please let's do this quickly."

"But I haven't finished cleaning the chimney!"

Santa laughed, dusted the soot off his red suit and said, "I believe you will find the job has been decently done for you. Maybe not to your high standards, but well enough to suit the master of this home for this year. Now pack up, collect your fee, and let's be off."

Peter quickly went up the shaft and saw that indeed it had been cleaned and most of the ash and soot had been removed. It took almost nothing to clean up the residue and pack up his tools. He saw the owner who paid him his promised amount and met Santa in front of the fireplace again.

They both went up the chimney and Peter was amazed that the large person before him went up with no effort. Santa went through the flue as if it were five feet wide. On the roof, Peter saw the sleigh and numerous reindeer. He was amazed to find his cart and tools already in the back of the sleigh.

"How do they not crash through the roof?" Peter asked wide-eyed looking at the animals covering the roof.

"We can discuss that on the way to my next house. For now, we need to get moving."

They went to another home and Peter waited in the sleigh as Santa completed his task. When they stopped at the next house Peter asked Santa, "You're delivering gifts here?"

Santa looked at his passenger and asked, "You have a problem with this?"

Peter pulled up his shirt and showed Santa the welt and abrasion on his back. "The boy that lives here gave me this tonight, for no reason other than he enjoyed it."

"Hmm, perhaps I should leave a present of a different kind."

"Yes, like a nice switch for his parents to use on him!" Peter was sneering.

"Not a bad idea," replied Santa. He reached into his bag and pulled out a couple golden birch branches. He went down the chimney and placed them into the boy's shoes.

Upon returning to the sleigh, Peter asked how he managed to pull exactly what he needed from his bag. Santa ho, ho, hoed and said that too, was a discussion for another time. They moved to a few more houses and at each one Santa asked the temperament of the children that lived there. He listened carefully, would nod his head and went down the chimney.

After the last delivery before they came to Peter's house Santa said to him. "I was thinking that it seems to me that naughty children could use a warning before Christmas, in hopes of them turning their behavior around before I visit on Christmas Eve. Maybe you could help me be my warning to the children who are misbehaving."

Peter looked at the man as if he was speaking an alien tongue. When he finally found his voice he asked, "You want me to travel with you? Each year you would come for me? You wouldn't mind being seen with me?"

"Of course not, although I quite thought that you might consider living at the North Pole with us. I think you would be more suited to your craft and kind up there."

"Who is us?"

"The other elves like yourself. Many elves have sought refuge up there long before you. We hear many tales of mistreatment by 'tall folk' as they call them. My wife and I are the only 'talls' who live there full time, although traders and certain friends to the North Pole are invited up on rare occasion and only more recently."

"My mother is not an elf, and I could not leave her alone here," Peter said, certain this was the deal breaker.

"And I would never ask such a thing!" Santa said with his eyes wide. "Exceptions can always be made and she would be most welcome. Obviously, as you are an elf, she probably has elven roots as well. Now let's go to your house and ask her."

Peter said, "I only know which are the nastier children in this town. How would I know who is undeserving in other towns and countries?"

"I can help you there. We have actually been discussing this very issue in the North Pole for some time. I have a couple elves up there who can help determine which are which for you. You would just help me dole out the punishments, instead of gifts."

When they got to Peter's hovel, his mother was greatly shocked to meet the living legend. Santa entered the house with a big bag of food. As he spread out the bounty, he told them tales of a magical land, along with an invitation to leave their poverty behind and become respected citizens in this place.

"Oh, Peter," she said with tears in her eyes, "just imagine living with others of your own kind. You could be a master chimney sweep up there!"

Santa smiled, "She's right, we could greatly use your services up there. You would be treated quite differently then sweeps are treated around here. All services and master craftsmen and women are highly respected."

They spoke a little longer and then Santa reminded them he needed to finish his rounds. "Tell you what, gather what you want to take with you, and I will pick you up at sunrise when I finish."

Peter said all he really needed was his tools, and that beyond what Santa brought them tonight, he and his mother did not have much in the way of personal items.

"I can fit whatever you'd like or need in my magic sleigh, but know you won't be returning, so make sure you have everything you want."

Hilda fell to her knees and kissed Santa's hand. He placed his other hand on the side of her head, smiled and said, "Your worries are in the past. You will be well cared for from now on."

And with that, he vanished from their eyes. He did not go up the chimney or out the door. They suddenly heard him call to his team outside and then the sound of bells fading as he left. For a little time, they stood and stared at each other with mouths agape.

Finally, Peter said, "I guess we should get packing."

"Not before I fill my belly with some more of this delicious food!" his mother cried out.

After they ate all they could, they gathered their meager effects. Peter recounted for his mother the meeting of Santa in the chimney, and how he told Peter of his plans for him.

"If you will be in charge of who is naughty, you would become the most feared being in all of Europe!"

Peter thought for a moment and was unsure about he'd feel being such a force of fear. He decided he would worry about that later. He shrugged to his mother and just said, "Yes, I suppose I could be, at that."

CHAPTER THREE

Just as the sun began to break over the horizon they heard the return of his bells. This time Santa landed in front of the meager hut of the Schwarztales. Santa and Peter placed the possessions of Peter and his mother into the sleigh that already contained the tools from before and Santa asked, "Is that everything you need?"

Hilda replied, "Well, that is everything we own."

Santa chuckled more to himself then said in a hefty voice, "Then let us be off."

They boarded the sleigh and Hilda clung to Peter with all her might as they were suddenly lifted from the ground by the reindeer and the man in front holding the reins. Peter grasped the side of the sleigh tightly trying to steady himself as he had done the first time he was lifted off the ground. He attempted to show no fear to his mother at their sudden ascension into the cold dawn.

Santa began singing a Christmas song, belting out the lyrics without a care in the world. He called back to his passengers and said, "Sing along if you'd like. I find music does wonders for calming the nerves."

"I sing about as good as I look," Peter said.

Santa glanced back at Peter. "So I should expect you can sing just fine. I don't see anything wrong with you that a warm bath and some new clothes wouldn't cure."

Peter stared incredulously at the big man. *Is he kidding? Doesn't he know I am the most repulsive being in our town, and maybe all of Europe?*

His mother squeezed his arm as if she was listening in on his thoughts. Though she had no clue what lay in store for her and her son, she believed with all her heart that it would be infinitely better than anything they left behind. Her only regret was that Karl wasn't with them. Though she secretly suspected that he sent this savior to them from heaven.

The wind became colder, and they huddled closer. As they began to shiver Santa called back to Peter and said, "There is a heavy blanket in my bag. Why don't you pull it out and throw it over yourself?"

Peter had been sitting with his boots on top of the bag and would have sworn it was empty. But when he went to lift it, he felt the bulk in it and pulled out the heavy woolen blanket Santa referred to. He flung it over his mother and him and were instantly warmed.

"Amazing," he said to Hilda, "I would have told you that bag was empty a moment ago. I was surprised that it hadn't fallen out of this sleigh before we got in, so I held it down with my boots."

"You forget who you are with," Hilda said, "This man of miracles is an enigma to all but himself."

What seemed to be but a moment later they approached the settlement that was the North Pole Village. As Santa gently set down the sleigh in front of a massive stable, a strong-looking elf stepped out of the dwelling and approached the team.

"Hello, Forrest!" Santa greeted the elf and gave him a powerful hug after he dismounted. "Say hello to our new residents. This is Peter and Hilda Schwarztale. Peter is a master chimney sweep and Hilda is quite accomplished in the kitchen. I am sure Denny and Pierre could use her skills."

Forrest walked over to the pair and gave them each a hug saying, "Welcome to our village. You are most welcome here."

It was perhaps the only time Peter had been hugged by another person that wasn't his parents. He enjoyed it, and wasn't put off in the least.

Hilda said, "We thank you. To say it is an honor to be here scarcely covers the feeling."

Forrest laughed and said to Santa, "I believe they will fit in nicely. And goodness only knows we could use a sweep in some of the houses around here. I know some particularly poor chimneys that could stand a good cleaning."

"My thoughts precisely," said Santa as he winked at Peter.

Santa left Forrest to tend to the reindeer and took the Schwarztales toward the main part of the village. As he walked with them a tall, older but pretty lady appeared and said, "There you are! I was beginning to get concerned. You are rarely this late on Christmas Day."

"My apologies my dear. I stopped to bring a couple new residents to our little world." he hugged Mrs. Claus tightly and quickly kissed her. "May I present Hilda and Peter Schwarztale? Hilda, Peter, this is my wife, Anne Marie Claus, the Chief Elf Organizer, or CEO, of the North Pole. She's the one that keeps me and everyone else in line."

She punched him playfully in the arm then turned to the pair and said, "Please, call me Annie. I am thrilled to welcome you here, and I hope you enjoy living here as much as we do." She gave each of them a big hug lifting them off the ground as she did so.

"We must say these are the warmest greetings that we have ever gotten. I think Peter and I are going to enjoy it here very much."

"Until your new house is built, you are welcome to stay with us." Annie told them.

"A new house? But how on earth can I pay for such a thing?" asked Peter, "I really do not have much more than what I earned tonight."

"With trade!" Annie said before her husband. "I assume you both have skills that can benefit the village in some way. You will help us and we will help you. That is the way this village works."

"He's a master chimney sweep, and Hilda is a gourmet cook!" Santa said with pride.

"A SWEEP!" Annie cried out.

"I wouldn't call myself a gourmet..." protested Hilda.

"Oh, but you will be once you work with Denny, Pierre and myself!" said Annie, as they led them toward the center part of town.

"And don't forget me! I am pretty handy, too!" Santa said acting put out.

"Of course you are, dear. Besides who would do all the taste testing if not for you?" They both laughed at this as they walked arm in arm. Hilda and Peter had never witnessed such warmth and affection between two people and were in awe of the couple.

As they turned a corner on the path the town came into view. Peter was dumbstruck at the variety of colors and architectural styles. Every color of the rainbow was in play, with a few extra thrown in. Hilda slowed trying to take in the full effect of it all. She gasped and said, "It is like no dream I ever dreamed. How beautiful."

The Clauses smiled and Annie thought this must have been their reaction when she and Santa first arrived at the North Pole all those years ago. They had come from the sky then, too, flying with five other elves in an airplane. As the outside world had no concept of this as yet, she was glad Santa didn't decide to have the elves bring them that way. It might have scared them to death.

"Come let's meet some of your new neighbors," said Santa.

"Santa, you must be exhausted. Why don't you head to our house and I will introduce Peter and Hilda around."

"I guess I am a little bushed. Alright, my love, you are better at this part than I am, anyway. I will see you later when you get home." After kissing his wife goodbye, he turned to his guests and said, "She will wear you out if you allow her. Don't be afraid to tell her when to stop. You do not need to meet everyone your first day. You will be here for quite some time."

The pair nodded looking out at the village before them.

Annie said, "You tend to yourself, I will take care of these two. Although, I doubt they have had much more sleep than you have."

Peter looked at Annie and said, "To be honest we haven't slept either, as we were getting our things packed for Santa's return."

"Well, then we should postpone this visit until you have had some decent rest," Annie replied.

"I couldn't possibly sleep right now," said Hilda, "I am much too excited!"

"Then here is my suggestion," said Annie, "I will take Hilda to meet Denny and Pierre, and you take Peter to our home to get some rest."

Santa bowed to his wife with mock formality, "As you command, my dearest lady. C'mon Peter, let us leave these two for some much-needed sleep."

Hilda shooed Peter with her hand and then rejoined Annie as she walked toward the dwellings before them.

When Peter saw the residence of Santa and Mrs. Claus,

he thought it was the biggest castle he'd ever seen. He had heard from his father about enormous estates in other places but had never viewed anything like this in his little town.

When he commented on this fact to Santa, Santa sloughed it off and said how Peter would see much grander than this in coming trips. They walked in and Santa led Peter up the stairs to a room with a large bed with down comforters and its own bathroom with running water. Peter had not seen or known about plumbing, so Santa gave him a quick run through of how everything worked.

Peter was astounded at the amenities. He looked around and then he stared at the gruesome figure in the looking-glass. At his home, they did not have mirrors. His father always said that they were not needed, and he was convinced they could steal one's soul if looked at too long.

Peter knew it was because of his looks, and his parents were just being kind. He looked at the grizzled reflection staring back at him. He had never gazed at it with such clarity.

Santa came up and put his hand on Peter's shoulder. "We only see the flaws in our reflection and never see the good that exists beneath the surface. You have a good heart. Try to see that, as we will."

"It is hard to look that deeply." Peter sighed.

Santa assured him. "With practice and confidence, I know you will. But for now, rest and refresh yourself. Just come down when you wish. When you get hungry, you will have plenty to eat, and when you are tired you may sleep as long as you wish. This is a time for you to be unconcerned about the future. We will deal with that after you and your mother have adjusted."

He left the room and Peter stood for a time trying to decide what to do next. Santa had recommended a "bath" in the large basin which was almost twice his size. He and his mother had a wooden tub that they would use occasionally, but this was massive compared to that. This also had hot water on command with just a turn of the spigot. This was unheard of in his village.

On the way over, Santa told Peter that he would see many things in the village that he had not observed or heard of before. He told Peter it could be many months until he witnessed many of the inventions and innovations of the North Pole. Every day would be a new adventure for him and his mother.

Peter decided that the bath would indeed be the thing, and he was still pretty dirty from his job. He turned the handles and was mesmerized to see that indeed the water flowed freely and was quite warm. He peeled off his clothes and stepped into the hot water. He felt the stress leave his body along with the dirt.

He washed the soot and grime out of his hair which was thick and matted when he got in. There were different soaps that Santa said would help his skin and hair. After nearly an hour in the large tub, he felt immensely better. He then put on some clothes that magically appeared on his bed and then rested his exhausted but refreshed, body on the down mattress. He was asleep in moments.

As Peter was stepping into the bath tub, Annie was introducing Hilda to Pierre and Denny. Denny was his usual affable self. He was as round as he was tall. A big round face with a small nose, bright blue eyes, and large dimples. His face was one, which you could not help but smile as you looked at him. He immediately welcomed Hilda into his kitchen and began showing her some of the modern conveniences that she would have never found in her village, nor anywhere south of where they stood presently.

Pierre was more aloof, and made the comment, "Mon Dieu, she is the big one, non?" Referring to her being a tall, something they did not see much in their top of the world retreat.

"Pierre, manners for our new guest, if you please." Denny reprimanded him.

"Pardon moi, mademoiselle," he quickly said, "I am not used to seeing many tall people around here."

"You are excused," said Hilda graciously, "I am in awe of your entire community, and just thrilled to be here at all."

She was as giddy as a new schoolgirl as Denny and Pierre introduced her around the kitchen. She was clapping with enthusiasm at each appliance and gadget they introduced. She swooned when they showed her how the ovens and ranges worked with just the turn of a knob. She had never imagined such ease and control for cooking.

"And it really keeps the temperature at a constant?" she asked.

"For as many hours as you care to, or is needed," replied Denny.

"How often do you add wood?" she asked, looking around for the wood pile.

"You do not. We use an entirely different heat source, which we will explain later," answered Denny. He was not sure he wanted to try to explain electric current or flammable gas to the new resident just yet.

Annie stepped in and said to Hilda, "Perhaps you would like to see your temporary quarters now?"

"I am almost too excited to want to leave, but I must

confess, this is all so overwhelming to me that I am getting a bit worn out."

"I understand, believe me. I went through a similar baptism by fire myself when Santa and I first arrived. And I bet you will sleep just as soundly as we did," said Annie.

"You will have plenty of time to play in the kitchen later. We will be teaching you all types of cooking and new techniques. We hope you will enjoy it as much as we do," said Denny.

"I can't wait! This looks to be so much easier and better than anything I have experienced before."

"Let's be off then," Annie led Hilda toward the door. "We need to get you rested up."

By the time they approached the last bend to the Claus' home Hilda was beginning to slow. But when the edifice came into view her excitement had peaked once again. "Oh, my goodness! Do I get to stay there today? I have never seen the like, although Karl told me such places existed. Now I know he is behind all this!"

She realized she was babbling to herself and apologized to Annie.

"Nonsense, I would have been disappointed if you were not pleased. You are welcome to remain here until your home is complete and we have everything set up for you," Annie said.

The tears streamed from Hilda's eyes. Her mouth moved up and down but no sound came forth. Annie gently placed her arm around Hilda and began walking them toward the house again.

Less than an hour later, Hilda had joined Peter in the same deep sleep world.

Sarah Buttons
Master Doll Maker

CHAPTER FOUR

Two days later, as was normal, the Clauses met with the Council of Elves, of which they were the President and CEO (Santa and Annie, respectively). It had become the tradition to give a report about the Christmas Eve journey and anything that was newly learned from the trip.

Each council member was anxious to hear the report, but they had learned that Santa had not returned alone this year, as in the past. Denny Sweetooth was also a member of the council and had been telling the others about how sweet Hilda was, and how the village now had a Master Sweep among them.

Though Denny was well meaning, some of the council members were horrified that another "tall" was not only brought to the village but brought here to live! As a rule, tall folks were not allowed to live in the village, with the exception of the Clauses.

When Santa brought the gavel down and called the meeting to order, their first question concerned the Schwarztales.

"My dear friends," began Santa Claus, "I merely addressed a wrong that had not yet rectified itself. Peter is an elf. There is no question there, plus he is a master craftsman in a field that this village was sorely lacking. His mother, I believe is just a taller elf than standard. True, she does not possess all the features that are more commonplace, however she is just barely five feet. She is the birth mother of Peter, and therefore, must have elven blood somewhere in her lineage."

Annie added, "I have spent the last couple days with them both. Peter is pensive, he has been ridiculed and tormented far worse than nearly anyone in this village. Hilda is a dear, and would make an exceptional addition to this village."

"It is my plan, with this Council's agreement, that I would use Peter as an assistant on the Eve of the Feast of St. Nicholas to dole out punishments to children who have been particularly ill-natured in their behavior," said Santa.

"We have talked about this, before," said Freida Cutinglass, "We cannot have Santa Claus distributing gifts and punishments to children when he is sought as the benevolent Gift-giver."

"Precisely!" Santa nearly yelled out, "I will now have an assistant that would take care of the punishments, and therefore would allow me to be separated as solely the Gift-giver. Moreover, Peter Schwarztale has a heart that can identify good children and those who are not."

"Truly?" asked Keeney Eagleye.

"Honestly, my friend," said Santa addressing the elf at the end, "I tested him several times and he told me specifically with the same accuracy you have. He knew precisely who was not deserving of a present just as you had said. He is the one."

"I knew others with the sight must exist," said Keeney, "We just haven't found them in our village."

"Who would want to admit it if they did?" asked Carrow Chekitwice. He was one of the oldest and wisest of the elves. He also was the Supreme Toy Maker who oversaw all of the production with Annie. "Truth is if I had the sight to see bad in people, I am not certain I would want to admit it."

"I do not believe he is aware he has it," said Santa, "I think he bases everything off his personal experiences. But he talked about the levels of evil in these children that only Keeney has discussed previously. I think he can be the face that would cause children to think twice about misbehaving."

"The stories that might spring up about him may change their behavior alone." said Ella Communicado, the elf in charge of communications between the elves of the North Pole and the rest of the world.

"Look at how the legends and stories have expanded about you now, Santa," said Frederick Salsbury.

Frederick was the elf in charge of commerce between tallfolk and the elves. He often traveled to other areas to procure the raw materials that were not available at the North Pole. He was one of the taller elves in the village, and like Hilda, more closely resembled a "tall" than an elf.

The discussion about Peter and Hilda continued for almost another half hour before Santa finally called for a motion. In the end, the Council agreed to allow Peter and Hilda to remain in the village and for Santa to begin grooming Peter for his role as Santa had laid out. Keeney and Santa would begin working together with Peter, as the rest of the village would create lodgings for their new chimney sweep and chef.

The Clauses had not mentioned the formality of the Council of Elves to the Schwarztales prior to the council meeting. They did not want to alarm them or cause them concern that they might not be able to stay after bringing them and introducing them around to others.

A bath and new clothes did much to improve Peter's overall appearance, but he gave a start to many that met him for the first time. Elves are always respectful to each other, and there were many that had been beaten, and worse, before escaping to the north. A couple asked Peter if that was what had happened to him.

No, he would say, he was just unfortunate enough to be

born this way. The elves would become embarrassed at their faux pas and quickly try to change the subject. Peter became amused at how the others reacted to him. Especially how hard they tried to look past his unsightly features. He decided that everyone's heart in this village was warm and genuine. For the first time in his life, he could be less fearful of other people's reactions turning violently toward him.

Some of the villagers began work on their new house. They asked the Schwarztales what they preferred in a particular color or style. Peter deferred the design and plans to his mother, who obviously was having the most fun she ever had with the suggestions and possibilities. It would be a small two bedroom, two bath dwelling, but would have more comforts than Hilda could ever envision, or imagine. It would also be more than twice the size of the shack they had left behind.

She decided on a violet exterior with a steeply sloping roof, similar to some others she saw. The elves decided on a building plot more towards the back of the village, closer to the woodland area. This was where the Clauses home and workshop were located. This made sense since Peter was going to be working closely with Santa, as his assistant for the Feast of St. Nicholas.

Peter had already begun cleaning chimneys and his talents were much in demand. He found the work much easier as few of the houses had more than one or two chimneys and were fairly straightforward to clean. No one in the village made any remarks as to the looks of Peter and everyone was accepting of him and his mother. Many went out of their way to welcome him as he pushed his cart through the cobblestone-style streets of the village. The streets were much smoother than the ones in his village and the stones were painted like peppermint swirled candies. It was almost dizzying to him if he looked down for too long at the pattern as he walked.

For the first time in his life, he found himself walking with his head up and taking in all the wonderful sights of the village and the people in it. He discovered that he smiled a lot more often because the other elves were smiling at him. How different was this world compared to the one they left?

After only a month, he and Hilda had moved into their new house. His mother cried with joy for almost two full days. She had never beheld a house like this, let alone dreamed that it would be hers. The kitchen and baths were a thing of wonder. Hilda had gotten quite used to working with appliances already and using the plumbing in the bathrooms at the Claus' home. But these were different, they were hers!

Peter was extremely busy cleaning various chimneys around the village and his list was already longer than his fathers ever was. He was welcomed at every house. He had to get used to all the welcome hugs as that was the custom in this village. In truth, he found it wasn't a hard custom to get used to.

It took Santa some time to find Peter, as he was moving around so much. Peter was working on his long list of houses requiring servicing. There was no rush to get them done in a special amount of time, but Peter wanted to help his now fellow elves, as they were helping him.

Santa finally spied Peter's cart in front of Sarah Button's home and workshop. She was Santa's Master Doll Maker. He knocked on the door and Sarah greeted him and then said, "Isn't it just wonderful, Santa? He is so good and is working so quickly! I will finally be able to get a good draft again and keep a fire going a good long time."

"Yes, yes it is, my little Sarah. However, as soon as he

finishes, I need to steal him away."

From the next room, a voice came, "I am finishing up now, and I can be at your house next if you need me that badly."

"It isn't my chimney that needs attending to. We need to go meet with someone about another matter," Santa replied.

Peter stuck his head around the corner with a quizzical look, "Oh?"

"It is time for you to meet Keeney Eagleye, and for us to discuss another job for you with the North Pole."

Sarah smiled at this. One thing the North Pole excelled at was information. News traveled faster than lightning from one end of the village to the other. No sooner had something happened in the Woodlands and the Manufacturing Center knew about it and so on. There were no secrets in the elven community. Sarah already knew what that job entailed.

A few minutes later, Peter was packed up and ready to leave with Santa.

CHAPTER FIVE

Keeney Eagleye was born in North America long before the white man settled in what would later become the British Colonies. He was born to a great warrior of his tribe. But, he was born different. He had sharply pointed ears. The great medicine chief of the tribe had declared that Keeney had evil spirits in his center and that the ears were proof of this. Allowing him to remain would bring a curse to all of their people.

Ordinarily, Keeney would have been put to death to save the tribe, but because his father was so feared as a fierce fighter, no one in the tribe was prepared to cross him. He, his wife and their cursed son were allowed to peacefully leave the tribe. This was tantamount to a death sentence for the whole family, but at least it would not start a war within the tribe.

So Keeney began his life in exile. During his second year, his mother was lost to a severe winter storm when a tree they were under collapsed onto their teepee. He had been wrapped and safe with his father, who was out hunting for game at the time and giving his wife a break from the toddler.

A couple months later, as his father was accepting his fate and preparing to die with his son, a strange group of nomads had come across the pair. After much struggle, the pilgrims made it clear to Keeney's father that they were going to a special place and offered to take his son with them where he would be accepted and raised as one of their own.

The warrior accepted and said goodbye for the last time to his son. The fate of one to the other was never known from that day on. But the migrants had kept their promise to the warrior. Keeney was raised in the North Pole Village. Here he was not only acknowledged but became a leader and served on the Elven Council.

Keeney had a special gift that was known to the other villagers. He could see into your soul. He knew quickly whether your heart was gentle or dour. Within a few moments, he could determine whether you spoke the truth, or were hiding something. It was Keeney that the elves used as the final test when they invited Kristopher and Anne Marie Kringle to the North Pole, before electing them to their post as Santa and Mrs. Claus.

He approved of them both. With Keeney's seal of approval, the Kringles were offered to become the gift givers of the North Pole the very next day.

And now he was going to meet with Santa Claus yet once again. And this time, he might be meeting someone more like himself. Although many elves shared common talents and interests, a few of them had particular gifts that were unique to them alone, or shared with a small few.

Aeon Millennium was one such elf. He had the gift of time travel. He had brought many of the elves inventions back from the future. This included the protective dome that allowed the village to remain safe and temperate in the inhospitable north. He had taught Santa another of his gifts. The gift of stopping or slowing time. It was how Santa was able to accomplish so much in an extremely short window.

Aeon had tried showing this gift to Keeney. After many tries, both elves had finally given up. For whatever reason, Keeney did not have the ability to either stop time, nor travel through it.

If Santa was right about Peter, Aeon would teach Peter this talent, too. It would be the only feasible way for Peter to accomplish Santa's plan on the Feast of St. Nicholas. But

Keeney was getting ahead of himself. He had to determine that what Santa surmised was true, and then they had to make the proposal to Peter, and he would have to accept.

There was a knock on the door, and Keeney opened it to the two men. He hugged Santa as was their custom, and then welcomed Peter. He grabbed Peter's forearm in his and gave a strong squeeze and shake. Though this was a foreign greeting to Peter, he went along and returned the same.

Peter had never met the likes of Keeney. With his dark reddish colored skin, long jet black braids and dark brown eyes, he was like no one he had seen before. He was a little taller and heavier than Peter. The two elves stood silently for a moment, as if sizing each other up. Keeney finally broke the silence and offered the two men a chair.

The building they were in was as strange as the look of this elf. Peter commented on the large tubular object projecting from the domed-roof as they approached. Santa had called it a "telescope" and said that Keeney was able to see tremendous distances with the apparatus. He said it was vital to his work with the North Pole, although he did not elaborate what that work was. The upper floor of the dome shaped dwelling contained the other end of the telescope along with books on every wall.

"So, I understand you are pretty good at reading people," Keeney began the conversation.

Peter looked at his host. "I really would not know."

"Have you ever felt a particular unease when you approached a person for the first time?" Keeney asked.

"Well, sure. Doesn't everyone? Especially when they look at me in disgust."

"No. Actually, most people do not. And those who do, it is more instinctual. With you, it is more of a surety. You can determine if a person is good or evil from a distance. Look into my heart and you will see I speak sincere speech." Keeney finished.

"I don't look "into people" as you say. I do not know how."

"Yes, my friend, you do," said Santa softly to Peter.

"You do not see your worth. We will need to change this or you will not be able to fully develop your gift," said Keeney.

"What gift? And I am but a lowly, misshapen chimney sweep." Peter shook his head as he said this.

"Your physical form has nothing to do with your gift! Look around you. Look at what our people have accomplished here. We are worlds more advanced than the tallfolk. Yet, we do not measure up to them in their eyes. They see us short in abilities because we are short in stature. This could not be further from the truth," Keeney said. "You are convinced you are of no worth because of what you have been told, and how you have been treated. It is time for you to release yourself from those false lessons."

Santa sat and nodded his head. "Keeney is right. Your beliefs are all wrong, period. They are no more valid than the belief the world is flat."

"And your true gift has yet to be put to use. Santa wishes to employ that ability far more than your chimney sweeping skills."

Peter looked at Santa, who continued nodding his head.

"I do not wish to seem dense, but I really have no idea what gift you are referring to."

Keeney stood and said to Peter, "Follow me."

He led Peter up to the second floor and to the tubular object that Peter inquired about as they came to Keeney's house. Keeney began looking through the small end of the telescope. He was turning several knobs and after a minute said to Peter, "Now, look through this lens with one eye and close the other. Look at the person you see there and tell me if you feel this person is good or not."

Peter wasn't sure he understood but did as the elf requested. He was amazed to see a man standing near a road. He was apparently waving his hands to other people going by. He watched the man for a couple moments. Afterward, he looked at Keeney and said, "He seems all right."

"Very well, let's look at another." Keeney resumed looking through the scope and turning knobs. He settled on an individual, "And this one?"

Peter looked through the scope, "His back is to me, I cannot... Wait a moment." Suddenly Peter shot upright and stared at Keeney. His eyes were wide. Peter said, "He is evil! He hurts people. A lot of people."

"There you see? And he did not turn around, did he? You got that from the waves he gave off. And although everyone does not fall into a strictly good or bad category, we can teach you to tell mostly one way or another who is good or not."

"Why would I need to know this?" Peter wasn't sure he wanted to run into people like the one he just saw. He could not imagine what good would come from meeting a person like this.

"So you can help me," called Santa from downstairs.

They moved back downstairs and took their seats.

"Help you do what? You said something about being a warning to children who were misbehaving. What has this got to do with warning you about bad-tempered boys and girls?"

Santa let out a loud "Ho, ho, ho!"

Keeney chuckled at the exchange.

"You would be my enforcer! You would bring switches

and warnings to those children who had a propensity to always do bad things. I would count on you to go before me into a town and leave the switches. This way both, I and their parents, would know who was not deserving of a present that year. It would also give them a chance to improve their behavior and become penitent. I would hope that they might still be deserving of a gift for Christmas. That is, if you and Keeney agree."

"What if they refused to be good at all? What if they enjoyed harming others and refused to repent their ways?" Peter knew of one young man like that in his town.

"What if you had a chance to stop the man you saw a short while ago?" asked Keeney, "Would you do something about it? What if you could protect all the people he harmed as an adult? Would you take action?"

"I suppose I would take them to somewhere until they mended their ways and became better people," Peter nodded.

"Like a prison?" asked Santa.

"I guess."

"How about a time, instead of place?" asked Keeney.

"Huh? I don't get what you mean," said Peter.

Santa interrupted, "Of course you don't. And it is not important right now. That is another meeting, with another elf, at a later date. For now let's just say you will be empowered to remove the more acidic people from society before they can do too much damage. For today, I just want you to contemplate what you are learning here, and what that would mean to you personally. I am offering you a fearsome future."

"Fearsome to me?" asked Peter, shifting in his chair.

Santa said, "No, you would be imposing the fear. Children and parents, both, would fear you and loathe you. You would have a lot of awful things said about you. People would terrorize children at the mere mention of your name. It is a frighteningly morose future."

"People already loathe me, I wouldn't lose anything there."

Keeney shook his head saying, "Not like the terror you would spawn after a few years of the punishment you would enforce. That is if, and once, you go down this path."

"Keeney is right. It will not be your looks that they will abhor, it will be what you do, and are capable of doing. Although I would venture a guess that interesting pictures of you will begin to surface after a few years. My own pictures differ radically from culture to culture, and most are unrecognizable to me. From that standpoint, I am not doing you any favors."

"Exactly why are you asking me to do this? Is being generous all the time finally getting the best of you?"

Keeney now laughed out loud and said, "Here we go!"

"It has been a long debate that my wife began many years ago," Santa sighed with the burden of having to relive the history once again. "She felt it was wrong that I rewarded all children equally, regardless of their behavior. She brought it up at one of the council meetings and it quickly spread throughout the village. Debates turned into arguments, and for the first time, serious disagreements could not be resolved. This is the closest I have been able to get a resolution that the whole village can get behind."

Peter looked at Keeney, "And you refused to carry this out?"

"Apparently it is not my place. And I cannot see into hearts as quickly as you are able. I help Santa with the naughty and nice list for Christmas. But there are things that you are better equipped for than me."

"Such as?" asked Peter.

"Time travel." said Keeney, matter-of-factly.

"What? What do you mean?" Peter's eyes were wide once more.

Santa intervened, "Enough for now. Since you now understand the basics of what I need and what the job entails, I would like you to go and contemplate the entirety of it. You can give me your decision in a couple days."

Peter thought for a moment and then said, "Actually I can give you my decision now if you like. My answer is no."

Keeney jumped from his chair and said to Peter, "You dare to refuse to help the great Gift-giver? After he brought you here and bestowed a great honor to you? I do not believe my pointed ears!"

Santa said, "Easy Keeney, it is his choice. Me bringing him here was not predicated on him doing this. And he is already helping many in our village, as is his mother." Santa faced Peter and asked, "I am curious though as to why you said 'no' so quickly?"

"All my life I have been rejected, mistreated and hated for my physical appearance. I have finally found a place where I am accepted and treated equally. The outside world will soon forget I existed if they haven't already. I am quite happy with that. I just cannot bear the thought of not only returning to that situation but increasing it throughout the whole world."

Keeney said, "But it is only one night a year!"

Peter replied, "But the effects would last the whole year through. Just as they do for Santa."

Santa held his hand up to Keeney stopping him from his next objection. "It is perfectly fine. I will need to find another is all."

"But you said Aeon told you he was the one!"

Santa glared at Keeney and said, "Enough."

With that Santa rose and they said goodbye to Keeney. He then escorted Peter through the door.

"Who is Aeon, and what did Keeney mean when he said Aeon said I was the one?"

"It is not important or relevant now. As for who is Aeon, you shall meet him in time, so there is no need to concern yourself with him today."

It was clear to Peter that all discussions on that day's topics were now closed. They walked mostly in silence back to where Santa had found him.

CHAPTER SIX

The next day Santa went to another house deep in the Woodlands section of the North Pole. The house itself had witnessed better days, but the garden around the home was immaculate and beautifully kept. Santa knocked on the door and heard a voice behind the house say, "C'mon in Santa, I am out back by the pond."

When Santa came through the house to the back yard, he said to the wild looking elf there, "I suppose you knew I was coming from your time travels."

"No," said the craggy old elf, "I knew it was you because you are one of only a couple elves who visit me and that you told me earlier you were going to take Knecht Ruprecht to see Keeney yesterday."

Knecht Ruprecht was the name used for Black Peter in Germany. This was one of the many names Black Peter would eventually come to be known by.

Aeon always had a disheveled look, something akin to a mad scientist. He sported a short beard that was as ragged as the rest of him. He had squinted eyes, that were difficult to tell when they were open as you looked at him. His face had so many lines around them, he resembled a municipal road map.

"Well, I do not think you should use that nomenclature for him. Things didn't go as planned. He said he would not do it. I do not think he is the one you thought you saw in the future."

Aeon looked at Santa with a sneer and said, "I see patience is still something you have not mastered. He will come around in time. The village will eventually do its bidding. Just let things take their course, and don't rush it."

"But when you told me that he would be the person to

do this, I assumed that we would begin the training this year."

"I never said that!" Aeon protested, wrinkling his face more, "I only told you who he was, and who he would become for you. Time is irrelevant. Surely, I have taught you at least that, by now."

Santa was quite used to the brusque nature of Aeon and knew he meant nothing disrespectful by it. He met Aeon through Frederick Salsbury many years back. It was Aeon that taught him how to stop time and move through the time continuum in order to accomplish his rounds in the shortest amount of physical time. Aeon also knew how to move across the past and future. That was one lesson he had yet to teach Santa. Aeon said there were too many complications and dangers involved with time travel, and he did not want the great Gift-giver getting killed attempting it.

Santa said, "I only want to return peace to the village. By Peter not accepting his mantle of responsibility, it will continue to cause disharmony throughout the North Pole."

"You worry too much. The village and its residents are not going to implode over this. And moreover, if you want Knecht to take on this mantle, he is going to need more than your request to do it. Otherwise, he will not do the task for as long as you need him. He has to see the need for it, himself. Until that happens, it won't mean anything to him personally."

"So you are saying the village is going to convince him to do this?"

Aeon approached Santa and put his hand on his shoulder and said, "My friend and I do not say that lightly, you of all people need to remember how unsure you were about taking on the...what did you call it? Oh, yes, the 'daunting impossible task' of being Santa Claus. It wasn't until you realized that first, it could be done and, second, you were the only one who could do it. I am certain Peter has some major issues he needs to rectify in his head before he decides that he is the one to accompany you."

"He doesn't want to be hated and feared anymore, he said. He wants to live a quiet life here in the village."

"I believe that may be his immediate concern, but again he will come around when he listens to the concerns of others. One year, at most two, I don't remember anymore, he will approach you with the idea again, and then we shall begin."

"Two more years! I don't know if I can wait that long! You know you could have told me this before you sent me to get him!" Santa was frustrated at the thought of two more years of the village bickering at each other.

"It would not have mattered," Aeon shrugged, "It will take Peter whatever time it will take him to come around. Some things in history cannot be rushed, much as you may wish. Be thankful you have him here now instead of another few years from now. That was when the original plan for you to meet him took place."

"So you actually had me change the future for this?"

"I prefer to think I just nudged it a notch."

"You told me that was a dangerous idea, and normally led to grave consequences."

"I had looked ahead on this and could see that nothing much changed. It just would have meant more misery for Knecht Ruprecht. His mother would not have made it. It would not have mattered much to his town as they had a sufficient number of sweeps. And the arguing would continue much as it has at the Pole."

Santa shook his head and said, "So you saved Hilda. All right, I accept whatever fate you tell me, as you already know the outcome. I just wished you would have prepared me better."

"If I had, you may not have tried to sell the idea as hard to him. And that may have cost you much more time for him to come around. This way he knows how urgently you want this to happen."

Santa sighed deeply and turned to go.

"Before you leave, I wish to move that large rock over there to this side of the pond. It will afford me a better place to overlook the pond and meditate."

"Very well. Anything for you professor."

In the days that followed, Peter was surprised how everyone already knew that he had been requested to assist the great Gift-giver and that he had turned him down flat.

No one accused Peter of anything wrong with his decision. Most thought of the daunting task that he had been requested to do, and did not believe they would want to take on that responsibility any more than he did. The conversations simply centered around what to do with the number of children that were less than deserving of presents.

Some had suggested that Santa should take switches along as sometimes both good and bad children were under the same roof anyway. Others said that the bad kids should be ignored completely. Doing so in the hopes that maybe they would eventually get the right idea. Still, others thought "to spare the rod was to spoil the child". And that would only insure worse behavior down the road.

A small few thought the gift giving should come to an end, altogether. They argued that Santa had done enough for the ungrateful tallfolk and their miscreant children. For the most part, they were a tiny minority.

Peter heard many of the comments and participated in several conversations. What he learned was that overall, the village mostly agreed that naughty children should be dealt with in some form or fashion. And although they understood and empathized with Peter for not wanting to be the bearer of those bad tidings, they were also against having Santa Claus deal with the problem.

So the disagreements raged on. Nearly everywhere Peter and Hilda went they heard raised voices about what to do with naughty children. None of the elves wanted to reward poor behavior. A few of the discussions got so heated, it led to elves avoiding one another to prevent permanent damage to their relationships.

All of these conversations and arguments worked at Peter's conscious. He began to feel more and more guilty about the riff taking place throughout the North Pole. There seemed no resolution in this except for him to take the mantle as "The Enforcer", and to straighten out the children who were causing all this strife, both in their own home and here in the North Pole.

Aeon missed his guess by a great distance. Not two years, nor one year later, but two short months after their last meeting, Peter knocked on the door of Santa and Annie Claus.

When Santa opened the door, Peter said, "I have two conditions."

Santa raised his eyebrows and said, "And they are?"

"First, I will only do this on the Eve of the Feast of St. Nicholas, and not Christmas Eve, or Day, or any other time. Second, I wish to restrict this only to Europe. I know you are now going to the New World and Asia. I also heard you were planning to add Australia and others. I will do this throughout

Europe, but no farther. One part of the world hating me will be quite sufficient, thank you."

Santa thought for a moment and then said, "Done and done. Now, why don't you come in and we will discuss this further? Annie just pulled a fresh batch of cookies out of the oven."

Peter walked inside and a grateful Santa Claus closed the door behind him.

Cocoa Nicenhot Cafe
Santa

CHAPTER SEVEN

Peter and the Clauses were getting to know each other better with Peter asking more questions than answering. He was curious about how Santa became Santa Claus and to learn more about the experiences he had. One of the more interesting aspects was how his appearance was perceived between Feast of St. Nicholas and Santa Claus.

"Actually the Feast of St. Nick is more about my illustrious ancestor Nicholas of Patara who became the first bishop of Myra. This is what we now are calling the country of Turkey. He was a wisp of a man compared to my bulkier side. However, their depiction of me is much rounder than my actual size."

"I keep telling you, dear, it's the coats and suits you wear," said Annie, "Because you need to keep warm, you look twice your actual size."

Peter smiled at Annie and asked, "That's another oddity, you are the Chief Elf Organizer of the North Pole, and yet nothing is known about you. How can that be?"

Annie laughed, "You might not believe some of the things Santa here has heard from children, and a few adults. For instance, when he talked to some kids once, he spoke of me and they all said he couldn't be married because he lives on a star. Another time, I introduced myself as Mrs. Claus to a young boy, and he said I couldn't be Mrs. Claus. He informed me that Santa is a ghost and ghosts aren't married."

Peter laughed out loud at the second story. This was the first time Santa heard him laugh and he thought it wasn't an unpleasant sound at all.

"And it doesn't stop with us," Santa jumped in, "I was talking about one of my red-nosed reindeer trying to explain

what caused that wonderful adaptation, and one of the
children interrupted me and said that he wasn't a reindeer at
all, he was a goat!"

"Well, I have heard lots of stories about you, and if I
remember right, one does involve you riding up from Spain on
a goat after arriving by boat."

"Yes, that is right, but this was in the American
colonies," explained Santa, "So you can only imagine some of
the things that will be said or inferred about you."

Peter shrugged, "You both are extremely different in
person compared to the tales, especially about Santa. I guess if
I look at what I am and will be doing one night a year,
compared to my life in the village, I can deal with it."

"That's the right attitude," exclaimed Santa, "Annie and
I are the same people we have always been, I just have a
specific job to do a few nights each year."

"A few nights?" asked Peter.

Santa explained about the International Date Line and
how the Christmas Eve journey was carried over two nights.
He then explained that his Latin American trip took place on
the Epiphany, which was January sixth, or the twelfth day of
Christmas. And of course, his trip that would now involve
Peter on the Eve of St. Nicholas on December fifth.

Once that subject was brought up again they began to
talk about the training that would need to be accomplished for
Peter to take his place along Santa' side.

The next morning Peter was asked to meet Santa at the
home of Sky Globetrotter. When he arrived, Santa was already
there and he and Sky were in a deep conversation. Sky
appeared to be a much younger elf than Peter. She had a

Scandinavian look to her with almost whitish blonde hair that fell to her waist. Her bright blue eyes were almost iridescent with hints of other colors dancing behind the blue. Peter became a trifle shy around her and would not say too much, as he did not want to seem uneducated or dumb to this beautiful lady.

Santa had watched Peter's reaction around Sky and had spied it before in others. He did not make anything of it. They finished what they were talking about, and then Santa explained to Peter why he wanted him to meet Sky.

"Sky handles all the traveling routes for me on my ventures. She is a meteorologist and can tell you what the weather will be like, which way the wind will be blowing and how strong, whether it will be raining or snowing, and most important, what will be the fastest route to make all your rounds."

"You mean to say that you do not just go in a straight line from village to village?" asked Peter.

"Mostly that could be true," Sky said to Peter, "But many times it is better to avoid certain areas because of jet streams and return to them later."

"I see," said Peter, though he did not have a clue as to what the pretty elf just said.

Santa cleared his throat and explained, "When we are flying, there are currents of wind which help me and the reindeer, or Amerigo, cover distances a great deal faster than on the ground. These currents are constantly changing and Sky here can predict which way they will be blowing."

"That is amazing," said Peter in a low voice looking at a map spread out on a table before him. The map showed arrows and swirls all over it.

"Those same currents also bring precipitation in the form

of rain or snow. So I can determine pretty accurately how to avoid storms, or what areas to visit first before a storm has a chance to get there."

"And she does a great job of keeping me, or getting me, out of trouble when I need it," said Santa.

"Umm, how can she get you out of trouble once you are already gone?"

"Another surprise you will learn about. We have wireless communications devices so we can talk to each other anywhere in the world," Santa explained, "You will meet with Ella Communicado later to be fitted with your device."

"Is that how everyone knows everything in this village? Does everyone have these already?" Peter figured this was how the news traveled so fast through the village.

Sky and Santa both began laughing heartily. Peter blushed red, but he thought Sky's laughter was music to his oversized ears.

"God forbid," Santa bellowed, "I can only imagine how fast news would race through the village if they did. It already travels faster than the speed of sound as it is. No, my friend, only a handful of us has need of these devices, which you will be one."

After that, Sky got down to explaining the basics of climatology and how things worked around the earth. Peter only understood about half of what Sky was telling him, but he felt he could listen to her all day.

After a time Santa interrupted the two and said it was time to get going to their next appointment. Peter thanked Sky for the information and said he would probably need to meet with her again to make sure he understood what he needed.

Sky said he was welcome anytime, and she would be

happy to clarify anything he was unsure about. Peter laughed and said that would be a long day for her. She gave them both a hug and sent them on their way.

Once they left Peter said to Santa, "How can she know so much?"

Santa wasn't sure he understood the question and said so.

"Well, I mean, she's so young, and a woman, where and when could she learn so much about all that?"

Santa ho, ho, hoed and said, "Sky is nearly 200 years old and she has been studying meteorology and climatology for more than seventy years!"

"What? That's impossible!" Peter exclaimed with wide eyes.

"Impossible or not, it is the truth. And women have an equal role in the North Pole as men. We do not distinguish between different sexes here. Anyone can do whatever job inspires them. And they can change if they ever decide to do so. We have some elves that are master tradespeople in several different fields."

"Yes, I had been told that. But nearly 200 years old?"

"You will find that living up in the North Pole you will hardly ever age. Several elves have lived many hundreds of years. We think it has to do with the magnetism of the Pole," explained Santa.

"The what?"

"I'll explain later. For now, we best pick up the pace, Forrest will be wondering about us."

"Oh, so we are heading back to the stables?"

"Yes, we need to figure out your transportation."

As they approached Peter saw the elf who was the first one to greet him in the North Pole. He was brushing a beautiful white stallion.

Forrest said, "Say hello to Amerigo, Peter. This is the horse you have heard so much about."

Peter walked up to Amerigo who nuzzled Peter as soon as he was in range. "He is the most beautiful horse I have ever seen."

Amerigo then turned his attentions to Santa, who reached up and began petting his long, luxurious mane.

Santa said, "We have developed quite a history together in a short amount of time."

"Short? I think not," said Forrest, "You two have been at it for over forty years now."

"And we plan to be at it a great many more, right boy?" The horse whinnied his approval. "Now Forrest, as we discussed, we will need a sturdy mount for our friend here to be the advanced guard for Nick's Feast."

"Well timing is everything, wouldn't you agree?" said Forrest with a big smile, "Just so happens that last year Buttercup and Amerigo had a son. And though only a yearling, I believe if he and Peter trained together, they would easily accomplish what you need of them."

Another elf was leading a mostly white horse with a grayish rump and tail over to the group. "And speaking of," Forrest said, "Peter, meet your new mount. We named him Avalanche. Of course, as he is now yours, you may give him whatever name you please."

"Avalanche. No, I quite like it. He is fabulous. I have never owned a horse before, this is going to be quite an experience."

"Well, we are going to need to teach you how to ride, and then how to fly. We needed to teach that second part to Santa and Amerigo, too. It is a bit tricky, especially in the beginning. You will need to come by here at least once a week, and probably much more as we get closer to December. We want you two to work as one before you ever leave the North Pole."

"You have our promise, right Avalanche?" though Avalanche was about two-thirds the size of Amerigo, he towered over Peter.

Forrest summoned his assistant, "We need to measure you for a saddle. Anything in particular you want? Santa loves bells, would you like some?"

"I think the quieter the better in my case. The last thing I wish will be to call more attention to myself that night."

"As you prefer. We will make it comfortable, but nondescript."

A short time later Santa announced it was time for their next meeting.

Peter could see Elf Mountain from anywhere in the North Pole Village, but he had not been there until that day. Santa and Peter took a large swing on cables to the top of the mountain where stood a large building called the Elf Resort and Training Center. Peter thought how he had discovered more things in the last few months than he had seen over his 27 years.

As they entered the resort, an elf that was seated on one of the large sofas stood and hugged Santa. "Frosty, my dear fellow. How have you been?"

Frosty said, "I am quite well, Santa, thank you." This elf had a thick and curly black beard. His hair was long and also curled at the end. He had hazel eyes that danced and were quite bright. These eyes were further accentuated by his eyebrows, which were almost as dense as his beard.

"Frosty, I would like you to meet Peter. He will be

accompanying me on Nick's Feast."

Frosty gave Peter a big bear hug and said what a pleasure it was meeting him.

"Peter, this is Frosty Evergreen. He is in charge of our mountain and forests around here. He will be the elf in charge of providing you with your switches."

Frosty said in a burly voice, "You just let me know what kind you would prefer, and how long I should make them, and I will see to it you have all you may need."

"Thank you, sir. But I really have no idea what I will need or how many." Peter looked at Santa for help.

Santa smiled at Peter and said, "You need not worry, Peter. It will come to you. If it is anything like me, it comes at night in your dreams and you wake up with answers you did not know you had questions for. I just want you to meet Frosty, and have him meet you."

"It is a great honor for me to serve the assistant to the great Gift-giver. I will be ready for your call anytime you need me." Frosty added a little bow at the end.

"Thank you, my friend, for taking time out of your busy day to meet us. You are excused to return to your many duties," said Santa.

Frosty hugged Santa goodbye and went on his way. Santa said to Peter, "This resort has some of the best cocoa in the village. Why don't we take a break and have a cup?"

Peter nodded and said, "Yes, I would like that Santa. My head is spinning with everything you have shown me today."

Santa ho, ho, hoed loudly, which made every elf in the lobby turn around and give a broad smile looking at the two of them. Santa caught this in his periphery and he also smiled inside. "My young apprentice, you have only begun to learn all the things you will need to know. You will be an exceptionally busy elf over the rest of your days, or at least until you decide not to be."

Santa led them to a little cafe in the corner and they ordered two mugs of cocoa. Santa requested a little mint in his. After they ordered Peter asked, "How do you mean until I decide not to be?"

"Someday you will wish to not accompany Santa Claus anymore. You may decide there is no joy or purpose in it. You may also tire of being viewed as less than an assistant. You see, although you are not my servant, I have been told some cultures will see you that way."

Peter interrupted, "Let me guess, Aeon?"

Santa nodded, "Yes, you will be thought of as Santa's slave in some countries. They do not understand that the very idea of slavery to us is something we abhor. Aeon also told me of a few other ways you will be viewed, but please don't ask me that now. You have enough to concern yourself with just learning what you will need to do this task."

"Is there any good that comes from this?"

"Absolutely!" Santa said loudly, "You change the lives of countless people young and old alike and mostly for the better. You become a celebrated tradition of the holidays. And you also remove some terrible people before they can do serious harm to a multitude of innocents."

Their mugs of cocoa had arrived. Santa blew on his and then took a sip. "Hmmm, perfect as always!"

The elf curtsied and then left.

Peter continued, "Well, I have already committed to you, and I am willing to accept my destiny. So when do I get to meet this Aeon?"

"We are going to his place first thing tomorrow," replied Santa.

"Good, because I promised to get a couple people's chimneys done by today."

"You know, you do not need to work so hard in the village. The elves would understand that you have commitments to me now."

"Santa, first I love doing chimneys, I always have, but now that the pressure is off of me to make enough so we can eat, I love it more than I ever have before. Second, as with you, if I make a promise to anyone, I keep it. So I want to do this, and I am enjoying doing it."

"What is it that you enjoy so much?" asked Santa, genuinely curious.

"It's dark and quiet, first off. It gives me a peace and lets me think without distraction. I can do the work with almost no thought since I have been at it for quite some time. I can think about other things, which according to what you have said, is going to be quite needed."

Santa nodded his head, "Indeed."

"Secondly, it may take a while for some to admit it, but every person and elf likes having a clean chimney. It is something they need and they all feel better once it is done."

"It is filthy work, though," said Santa.

"Dirt can be washed off. And here that is easier than I could have ever have imagined. I love my daily baths. My mother teases me that I am the cleanest elf in the village, now."

"I had noticed that you have been a good deal more presentable than when I had met you."

Peter shrugged, "Well, the new clothes everyone is bringing sure helps. I may be the same physically grotesque being outside, but at least I am clean and not in tatters, anymore."

"You really should ease up on yourself," Santa admonished Peter, "I have come across far worse than you in my travels. I have run across hunchbacks, burn victims, lepers, and people with serious diseases that would have you look like the winner in an 'Elf of the Year' contest. Besides, Sky wasn't repulsed by your looks."

"Now why would you bring her up?" Peter shot at Santa.

"I am not blind, I saw how you looked at her. She didn't seem to mind looking at you, either."

"Pshaw! I was just intrigued with what she had to say. I find wind currents and weather interesting is all. Besides I could never be serious about a girl."

"Oh? And why is that?" Santa asked with a raised brow.

"What if I were to get married and have children? They might all have my cursed looks and be rejected as I was."

"Or, they may take after their mother more, and they would certainly have a caring father to look up to. Further, if they were in the North Pole, they would never be rejected or mistreated. You should realize that by now."

For the first time in his life, Peter dared to think of living a more normal life with a wife and family. He began to smile and then thought of the way he would be viewed outside the North Pole. He shook off his reverie and just said to Santa, "These are thoughts and concerns for another time. I have much to learn and prepare for. I must keep my attention where it is needed."

Santa simply said, "As you wish, but I wouldn't dismiss it completely. You have a right to your happiness as much as any elf."

They finished their cups of cocoa and left the cafe, and each other, until the next day.

CHAPTER EIGHT

Aeon was doing what he loved best to do. Tending to his garden. This always brought him the greatest peace. It was something he absolutely had to do when he returned from one of his jaunts to the future.

Even though he returned yesterday, he needed to relax more than usual. He was rarely happy about what he saw on these trips. He certainly wasn't impressed with the road humanity was taking. In spite of all the advanced technology and impressive gadgets he would come across, they had not mastered the simple act of living with each other.

Quite the contrary, he now pondered, he felt they had grown ever more distant. They rarely socialized or met in person. Everything was done through cyberspace and except through artificial intelligence, they rarely spoke at all. And since telepathy had not been discovered, and was not likely to be at this pace, there was a tremendous amount of miscommunication. That did nothing to help keep the peace.

He heard the knock on his door and thought for a moment about ignoring it. He knew who it was, and why they were here. After his jaunt yesterday, the last thing Aeon felt like doing was working in the time continuum once more. The knock came again, followed by Santa's voice, "Hello Aeon, are you home?"

Patient as always, aren't you Santa? Aeon thought. Instead of saying that however, he answered, "I am in my garden, please take your time joining me there." He finished tending the flowers he was working on and began to move toward his ramshackle house.

As Santa and Peter came out the back door, Peter was amazed by the garden before his eyes. He gave out a low whistle and said, "This is incredible! I have never seen so many types of flowers in one place. How do you keep the temperature so perfect to grow so many varieties?"

"I have a mini greenhouse dome over the garden to give the perfect ambient climate, just enough moisture and the right amount of partial sun to entice flowering," Aeon answered.

"I would spend all my time here if I had such a garden," said Peter.

"And he does," said Santa with a snide grin.

"It beats spending it with people, at least the plants don't give me nearly as much trouble," replied Aeon, "But we are not here to discuss botany. We need to teach you something else."

"I am a little concerned that I may not be smart enough to learn how to control time," said Peter.

Aeon looked mildly surprised.

Santa said, "Keeney spilled the beans."

Aeon nodded, "You are and you will. I have watched you do it, and that is all you need to know. If you are like this one, I will pull my hair out trying to keep you from asking pesky questions for which you do not need to know the answers."

"Who would notice if you did pull out your hair," taunted Santa.

Peter looked at Aeon and said, "I only need to know what you need to show me. And if you say I will learn, then I shall try to do so quickly so you may return to your garden."

Aeon paused and looked Peter over solemnly. He said, "Oh, I like this one, I truly do. Santa, why can't you be more like him?"

"Because you wouldn't feel as appreciated if I wasn't asking you for more information that I know you are hiding."

"Try me some time. Okay, let me begin by saying you need to forget everything you ever knew about time," began Aeon.

"I don't know anything except how to tell what time it is," replied Peter.

"Good. You need to think of time as a moving river. We are all floating on it and it is taking us down its current. Look at the way the waterfall in my garden flows. Now, what if you could turn off the current?"

"It would remain in one place," answered Peter.

"Right! So the question becomes how to stop the current and keep it in one place?"

Peter shrugged.

"You need only have the will to stop it. Pay attention." Suddenly the waterfall stopped in mid-flow. The water hung in midstream. Peter stared with his mouth agape. Aeon continued, "Now close your eyes and picture the river of time. See it moving across the landscape. Now picture yourself like a dam holding back the river. Start to slow the current a little at a time..."

They worked on this for the next hour. Aeon demonstrated a few more times how it worked, first with himself, and then he had Santa show him. Peter wasn't able to stop time but did manage to slow it a couple times. Aeon told him that he got further than most, and that was as much as he could hope for in one day.

He told Peter he wanted to work with him daily for the next couple weeks, at least. "If you do not work on this every day, and all day, you will not make any progress."

Santa said, "He had me coming up here every day for months at first."

"You were more stubborn to teach, that's why. I think

Peter will have little trouble catching on to this."

Santa feigned hurt feelings but knew Aeon was right. He had more trouble accepting the concept of stopping time after he had done it. He remembered being there with Frederick the first time he froze time. He had frozen Frederick at first. But he did not believe it after he accomplished the act. Santa also felt that Peter would catch on sooner.

After another hour, they decided to break for the day. Santa told Peter that he could work on it all day if he'd like and that it didn't matter where he was. Aeon agreed and told Peter to meet him there the following morning and they would work together until Peter was able to do what he needed.

Peter went back to his home and was trying to stop time as he walked. He wondered if he needed to remain stationary in order to freeze everything else. He would ask Aeon that tomorrow.

When he got to his home, there was a note from his mother saying that she had gone to assist Denny Sweetooth and Pierre Gastonlove with a large luncheon they were putting on for one of the assembly plants.

Peter had witnessed the remarkable change in his mother since arriving. She looked and acted twenty years younger. He had only known her barely getting through each day. Always tired, she never ate much and moved as if dragged down by a huge weight.

This woman that lived with him now was entirely different. She bounded from place to place with an endless energy. She was laughing and smiling all the time. Her voice was stronger and she related the events of the day to Peter as if she wanted to go back and do them all over again.

Peter was extremely happy for her. He knew that he was as changed as she was. He did not feel the dread he had felt at their former village. He knew nothing had improved with his looks, but he was less self-conscious about it if only little bit. People did not make fun of others here. Everyone was respected and judged by their abilities. And everyone always was willing to pitch in.

Speaking of pitching in, he had promised to work on the chimney of Coco Nicenhot. She was an important elf as she was the Chief Cocoa Maker and reported directly to Santa Claus. She also was in charge of the various cocoa cafes that were around the village. She had asked Santa to check Peter's schedule, as she was concerned about the part of her chimney she used over her stove constantly.

Peter gathered his tools and placed them in his cart. The elves had offered to make him a new cart, but this was his father's and Peter had fond memories of he and his father with this cart. Plus it carried his father home that last day they worked together and he felt that part of his father was in that cart with him.

He sauntered off to Coco Nicenhot's home, and before he arrived he could smell the cocoa wafting out of the house. He knocked on the door and a moment later a smallish elf with a broad smile on her face opened it. Coco had brunette locks that ran down both sides of her head. She was a little plump, but he thought fat might be too severe a term to describe her. She welcomed him in and said how glad she was he could find the time to come by.

"Oh well, I am not as busy as all that," he said, realizing he was now smiling, also.

"That isn't what I have heard! You are training with Aeon and Forrest, learning about weather from Sky, and doing chimneys. That would fill up anyone's day."

Peter blushed and then mumbled, "I guess so."

"You are much too modest Peter Black. Here let me show you my problem." She led him to the flue over the stove and oven. "It doesn't seem to be drawing well at all."

He felt the range to see if it was cool, which it was. He said, "Funny, I could have sworn I smelled cocoa cooking coming up here."

"I made a batch a little bit ago. It is still quite warm if you'd care for some."

"Perhaps later," he said, "Let me work on your problem first. How is the draw in your fireplace?"

"It seems to be all right. This is my bigger concern since I use it all the time."

When Peter was approaching the house he saw the two chimneys sticking out above the roof. This was one of the older houses. It had used wood burning stoves before the more modern stoves were built and installed. He marveled at the inventions they had in the village compared to "the other world" as he and Hilda now called it. He wondered just how long ago this had been cleaned out and asked Coco.

This time Coco blushed with embarrassment. "Can we just say it has been too long, and leave it at that?"

Peter chuckled and nodded, "Okay, fair enough."

He began pulling out his tools and went to work above the stove. The initial opening was rather sticky and a bit messy. Coco apologized and swore to him that she had cleaned it as soon as yesterday. He waved it off and said, "I would have been surprised if it had been anything other than the way it is."

He scraped away as much as he could and went further in. Peter disappeared into the flue and Coco thought he had vanished. As Peter got further in he hit a big pocket and figured he had found much of the blockage. He realized with dread that in his rush to get cleaning out Coco's work area, that he hadn't taken his usual steps to prepare for the mess that was about to fall out of the smoke stack. As a large piece broke loose he quickly held up his hands toward the broken creosote and...

It stopped falling in mid-air. It had come to a complete halt. Peter stared at the floating debris before him and regained his wits. He scurried down the chimney and pulled out his protective tarps and laid them over the stove and floor. When he had gotten everything situated he looked up the flue again. Just as suddenly as it had stopped, the dirt and soot tumbled forth out of the chimney and onto the sheets.

"Now how did I manage to do that?" Peter asked himself out loud. He further wondered if he could do it again. So he crawled back into the chimney and moved ahead of where he was working. For the next thirty minutes, he worked through the rest of the firewall, always trying to stop debris as he had done before, but with no success.

By the time he finished, he wondered if he had really prevented the free fall before, or was it his imagination. But no, he was sure of it. Apparently, whatever he did, he wasn't able to replicate a second time today. But he did it. He was nearly euphoric at the thought and could not wait to tell Santa and Aeon.

After a quick review and cleaning of Coco's other firebox, he and Coco sat down with a mug of hot chocolate and he told her what happened.

"I have never understood that grumpy sorcerer, and although I appreciate all the wonderful things he has provided to our village, he is not the most approachable elf here," said Coco. "I certainly do not understand how one can control or stop time, and I would be scared stiff to try it. I keep imagining what could go wrong."

Peter said, "I can imagine quite a number of things, myself. But to be fair, I can see several going right, too. For instance, take the mess I just saved myself here."

Coco laughed and said, "So I suspect everyone will be held in suspended animation while Peter does his chimney sweeping from now on."

Peter smiled and said, "Not as a routine course, although that is an interesting premise." He laughed at the thought.

Shortly afterward he left for home. Peter was now confident that soon, like Santa, he would be able to control the time at will.

CHAPTER NINE

The next day when he told Aeon, he did not receive the feedback he'd imagined. Instead, Aeon just said, "I know, I felt it."

"You know when the time has stopped? By anyone? Including Santa?"

"You're babbling, and yes. What's more, it takes a great deal to catch me in the warp, but I can see around me when things have ceased moving."

"How is it you are not affected?"

"I am not, and that is all you need to know. Now show me how you can stop time."

Peter looked down at the ground and said, "I haven't been able to stop it since that instance. I have been trying."

Aeon grumbled, "Obviously not hard enough. What were you thinking about when you did it before?"

"I was worried about the huge mess I was about to make."

"Then concentrate on that," said Aeon, "Think about what a mess will ensue if you do not learn how to do this." He chuckled at his own joke.

"Hilarious," although Peter was not amused, "I am unable to turn it on or off as yet."

"We need to work on this. All right, you were evidently stressed over what was going to happen. So use that for now. Think about everything that is going to happen and all that could. How do you prevent it? For instance..." Aeon reached up to a cup on the shelf and knocked it off.

The cup hit the floor and shattered. Aeon looked at Peter and said, "Why didn't you stop it?"

Peter looked at the elf with frustration and said,

"Because I didn't know what you were doing!"

Aeon said, "You didn't know about the soot and ash that was about to hit the floor yesterday, either. If you did, you would have prepared for it. You need to be able to stop time instantly like Santa and I do. Santa has people walk in on him all the time. He has to be able to freeze them immediately, or he would never get his job completed. It has to become as natural as breathing, and just as unconscious."

"I was hoping you would be pleased that I stopped it at all."

"I will be pleased when I see you do it on purpose, and not by accident. I will also be pleased when you can do it at will, whenever you wish to. Now clean up that cup, and then let's get started. Darn, that was one of my favorites, too."

An hour and a half later, Peter had only managed a moment of time suspension and lost it almost as quickly as he stopped it. Aeon said that was enough for the day and that Peter should keep working on this throughout each day on his own. Peter did learn that he did not need to be frozen himself to stop time and that he could prevent himself from falling, or slow his descent, once he mastered the time continuum.

Peter left Aeon's and went off to his next lesson with Forrest. Peter had always enjoyed being around animals, as they were not judgmental like people were, but learning to ride one was going to be an entirely new experience.

When he arrived at the stables, no one was around. He called to Forrest but there was no reply. He walked over and checked out the reindeer. He saw the glow from the four red nosed reindeer at the far end. He walked over to a stable marked "Torch". Inside was a coppery colored reindeer with a bright red beak. The reindeer walked over to Peter and he began stroking his neck. His nose got brighter and Peter said,

"Easy there fella, let's turn that down a couple notches."

As if the reindeer understood, the light diminished to a much lower level. Peter kept petting the deer until he heard noises outside the stable. As he moved back outside he could see Amerigo coming up the lane with his bells ringing and Forrest at the reins.

A moment later, he saw Avalanche following with another rider on him. Forrest introduced Pepper Haystraw to Peter once he dismounted Avalanche.

"That's a fine horse you have there, Peter," said Pepper. "I don't think you are going to have any trouble learning to ride him."

Forrest said, "I am going to have Pepper teach you how to ride, and then I get to teach you and Avalanche how to fly."

Pepper got Peter up on the saddle and began teaching him the basics of rein management and how the reins steered the horse. Peter who always wanted to learn to ride was a willing student. Soon after, he was leading Avalanche around the paddock in front of the stables as if he had been riding for days.

Peter noticed the large brass hooks on the backsides of the saddle and asked their purpose. Pepper replied, "Those are for your use. One is to carry the bag of switches you will have with you, and the other is for the children you will need to carry away with you."

"You seriously think I am going to carry off children? What children would be so horrible that they should need to dragged away from their homes? And just what would I do with them once I have them?"

Pepper shrugged and said, "We just did what we thought Santa might want for you. You would need to discuss this with him. He said that Aeon told him what your role would be in history and that removing particularly bad children was part of it. We just expected this would help."

"Well we will have to see about that," said Peter, "In the meantime, I will not need them and I am more concerned about sticking myself with those, then what I will be carrying with me. Is it possible to remove them until after I have learned how to fly?"

"Anything for Santa's Assistant," Pepper said, "When you finish today, I will see to it."

Thinking about what Santa was expecting him to do, he'd lost his enthusiasm to ride anymore that day. Instead, he knew where he needed to go next. He said as much to Pepper and dismounted off Avalanche.

It was a long hike to the top of Elf Mountain. One of the things he learned in his discussions with Aeon was that he would be able to move from one place to another using the time continuum. He thought that would be particularly useful for jaunts like this.

By the time he reached his destination he was out of breath. He waited until he was able to catch it again before knocking on the door. Keeney Eagleye opened the door and invited Peter in. Peter did not waste any time and asked Keeney about what was bothering him.

"Why will I need to take children away? I have met some pretty nasty cretins in my village, but I cannot imagine tearing them from their homes. How would their parents react? I am sure they would not understand."

Keeney listened to the elf sputtering his concerns and felt bad for him. He had also been told of Peter's contribution to history. He heard of how Peter would be viewed in some civilizations and knew it wasn't pretty. It was far worse than Peter's actual looks.

"You will save many lives. You will also prevent great suffering in many instances. But most importantly, you will know in your heart why you will need to do what you do, and when you will need to do it," said Keeney.

"Many of these children are the same size as me and some are much bigger! How am I to carry them anywhere?"

Keeney said, "Many things that you do not know now will be made clear to you in time."

Peter said, "Like how I will know who is good or not?"

"You already know that. You just need to trust your instincts and feelings."

Peter was frustrated at hearing the same things again from Keeney without any substance. Keeney could see this and brought him to the second floor again. He told Peter, "This time you look through the telescope and look at the different people. Just watch them and get a sense of who they are, how they live, and most importantly, what is in their heart."

He taught Peter how to use the dials and focus in on different people. He told Peter to take deep breaths and let his mind run free as he observed them. Keeney told him to not look for the good or bad in someone, but just to become part of them for a moment or more. "Then," he said, "You will know all that you need to about them."

Peter did as he was instructed. He watched and scrutinized several people. At first, he could not determine a thing about them. But as he slowed his breathing and calmed himself, he began to pick up small nuances about them. He quieted his thoughts and studied each subject. Then he began to feel what they were like, and he could tell the kind of person they were.

He saw their good qualities and bad. He learned their temperaments and knew by watching them how they would react to situations in their lives. He realized that he knew more about them than they knew themselves. It was at once a frightening and empowering feeling.

After several minutes went by, he stepped away from the telescope.

"You know now why you must do what you are empowered to do," said Keeney, "You as the gardener must remove the weeds that would destroy the garden."

"I did not witness anyone that deserved to be removed from civilization," said Peter.

"Probably not in that brief time, no, but I am sure you will in your travels," Keeney said, "One can only hope that you will be able to find and remove the 'black hearts', as I call them, before they can do damage to others, as has happened in the past."

"If this has been so badly needed, why haven't you had someone take care of this before?"

"We needed to find the right person. You have the ability to see from your heart into others. We could not proceed without you."

Peter just nodded but thought that he was no different from anyone else. Didn't everyone have the ability Keeney spoke of?

As if reading his mind, Keeney said, "Almost no one can see into another person's heart, not even Santa. I can do it, but not nearly as competently as you. You are far faster in your assessment and can see more clearly than I can."

"How do you know this? Perhaps I am no more skilled than you are," Peter rebuffed.

Keeney told him that just as he could see strengths and weaknesses in others, he could see the strengths of Peter. "I knew immediately you were better suited for this task than I ever would be."

Before Peter left later, Keeney invited him back to begin working on a list for Nick's Feast later that year any time he cared to visit.

CHAPTER TEN

Peter began his cycle of riding, viewing, and learning about climate and the time continuum. In between these, he worked on various chimneys and assisted where he could. Peter was rapidly considered one of the hardest working elves in the North Pole.

He was progressing nicely and had already taken to the sky with Avalanche. Forrest and Pepper were impressed as to how well he was doing and had commented on his progress. Perhaps he was feeling a tad overconfident. He was heading into the sky on Avalanche when it happened.

After a perfect lift off the ground, Peter's boot got tangled in the stirrup and he panicked. He lost his balance entirely and slid off the saddle. He was only a little way up, perhaps twenty feet, but he was terrified. Then everything stopped.

Peter floated to the ground and stood up. He saw Forrest pointing to Avalanche, and Pepper with his hand across his mouth. They were frozen there. He looked up at his mount hanging in mid-air looking back to where Peter had fallen off.

Everything around him had ceased moving. There was no sign of motion. He saw Amerigo with his head outside his stall just staring forward. Peter concentrated on releasing the continuum but nothing happened. He became frightened. What if he was unable to reverse the spell he had placed everyone under?

He remembered that Aeon had said that he was unaffected by the stoppage, and Peter ran off to seek his help. Luckily, Aeon's cottage was not far from the stables. When he got there he banged on the door. There was no answer. He banged on the door once more. Again, nothing from the other side.

He hoped that Aeon might be in his garden and couldn't hear him, so he entered and went through the cabin. He went out the back and spotted Aeon halfway up the garden. He moved toward him and saw that he, too, was not moving. Nor was the water in his pond. There was a butterfly suspended in mid-wing a few feet from his teacher. His despair was almost overwhelming. How would he ever be able to set things right? Is it possible that time would rectify itself, in time? He thought of the irony of that question.

He was jumping around trying to figure out what to do when suddenly he heard a sneeze. He spun around and heard Aeon say, "Nuts, I wanted to see what you would do next."

"You aren't stuck in the continuum?"

"I told you, I am rarely affected by the alteration of time. We are old friends, time and me, and we have special agreements. You, on the other hand, are just a meddler."

"Can you fix this?" pleaded Peter.

"The more important question is can you?" answered Aeon.

"Obviously, I cannot, which is why I ran over here!"

Aeon held up his hand. "First, you need to take control of your fear. Stop and take some deep breaths. Slow yourself down."

"I'm afraid! What if I can't release these people? What if this happens when I am out there on the Eve of the Feast of St. Nicholas? What would I do?"

Aeon waited until Peter finished without answering. Finally, he said, "Done? Good. Now take a few deep breaths. Pay attention. You have not altered anything. In fact, just the opposite, you have stopped everything from proceeding. Here, see this butterfly?"

He reached over to the insect and carefully took it from its place. He brought it over to Peter and placed it in the air between them. "Now, when you release time, this will be the only change made. Unless of course, you would like to interfere with a few other things for sport?"

Peter looked at his teacher horrified and said, "No! I just want everything to start again!"

Aeon shook his head saying, "The sooner you calm yourself, the sooner your wish will be granted."

Peter closed his eyes and took a couple deep breaths. He listened to his lungs fill and release the breath. He concentrated as Aeon had shown him before on slowing his blood flow and clearing his mind. After a few moments, he was calmer.

"Good," said Aeon, "Now concentrate on the time continuum. What were you doing when you stopped time?"

"I was falling," said Peter.

"In a chimney?" asked Aeon.

"No, through the air. I had fallen off Avalanche, my horse, as we were taking off. I panicked and was scared I would be injured so I stopped my fall by freezing time."

"Did you stop also?"

"No, I kinda floated to the ground. When I stood up, I could not start the continuum again. I wasn't in control."

"You are always in control." Aeon stated, "You stopped time and you can start it again. You just need to undo what you did. No one else stopped it to slow your fall. Think!"

Peter took himself back to when he slipped from the saddle and thought about what he was thinking. He thought about how Aeon had told him that he could prevent himself from falling using the continuum. He thought about how he had called on that ability so he wouldn't get hurt. He was focused on the continuum as he had in Coco's chimney when he stopped the debris. At that moment he realized Aeon was right. He controlled time, not the other way around.

The next moment he heard the water in Aeon's garden flowing. When he opened his eyes he saw the butterfly floating nearby where Aeon had placed it.

"Although not intentioned, this was a huge step in your training," Aeon was actually smiling.

"I have never been so scared in my life," said Peter. He was feeling exhausted from the ordeal.

"That is often how we learn. The most important part was that you overcame your fear and returned things to normal."

"Oh my gosh! Avalanche! I left him in mid-air without a rider!" Peter jumped to his feet.

"He will be fine," assured Aeon, "But go see to him, and then return to me. Otherwise, I will not have your concentration. We need to discuss this more and work on your training. This was a big step for you, and I want to build on it before you forget it." Aeon knew he would not be able to teach Peter anything unless he was certain everything had returned to normal and that his horse was unharmed.

Peter agreed and ran off to the stables. When he arrived Pepper and Forrest called to him.

"What happened?" Forrest yelled out, "One minute you were falling off Avalanche and the next you disappeared."

"Where did you go?" said Pepper, "Did you land somewhere else?"

"In a matter of speaking," Peter said embarrassed, "I kinda accidentally stopped time and went to get help."

Forrest laughed, "I'll bet Aeon liked that one!"

"Yes and no. He said it was a big step for me, but insists

I return to go over what I did. I just came by to make sure Avalanche was okay."

"He's fine," said Pepper, "He was a bit confused at what happened to his rider, but he touched down easily and trotted off to his stall. I was just coming back from removing his saddle. You can go reassure him if you'd like."

Peter walked over to his steed. The horse moved to nuzzle him and Peter said, "Hey buddy! Sorry about the scare. I will try not to let that happen again. Good news is I think I know what to do if it does." He stroked the horse a few times and then headed back to Aeon.

On the way back, he thought about what he had done and thought to stop time. As he walked he concentrated again on the process. He watched as a bird stopped in mid flight. And he knew he had caused it. He watched as the bird began flying once more. He did this a couple more times as he walked to Aeon's house.

When he got there Aeon was waiting for him. "Having fun?" Aeon asked Peter, "Any time you want to quit playing with the continuum, I would appreciate it. You are as bad as Santa was when he finally learned how to stop time. He was forever starting and stopping things. I hope you are not going to do that, too."

"I thought you would want me to practice. I think I finally figured it out!" said a hurt Peter.

"And practice we shall, but there are many more things I must teach you beyond the stoppage of time. These are things only you and I will know."

"And Santa, you mean," said Peter.

"I always say what I mean!" snapped Aeon, "What I am about to show you Santa does not know. Nor does he need to know. This is for you and your position only! You are not to talk to anyone about what I am about to teach you, not even your mother."

Peter stood silent. He could not fathom knowing something that the great Claus, himself, wouldn't know. He was excited and nervous at the same time. "I am your servant," was all Peter could say.

Aeon began, "After I am convinced you can stop time on demand, we will begin the next part of your training."

For the next hour, Peter showed Aeon how he could now control time. Aeon also showed him how he could narrow the stoppage of time to a small area. He explained that holding it in one place would have a type of spring effect that would snap that area into the present when released. As rubber bands had not been invented yet, Aeon could not use a simpler example.

This lesson was the most important in the training Peter would need. Once he was able to accomplish this, Aeon would be ready to show how this was relevant to his job.

"Now we can put someone into a time lock and keep them there as long as we care to," Aeon said, "So if you come across someone that you wish to place in a time prison, you will be able to do so, and then release them on command, without them ever aging a day."

"I take it this is for the undesirables I am to seek out and punish?" asked Peter.

"These 'undesirables' as you call them will need to be rehabilitated before they harm civilization as a whole. Otherwise, they will never be worthy of society, and could cause much harm to it."

"Who is supposed to feed and take care of them, once they are locked away?" asked Peter.

"You are not getting this. The whole point is that they

will remain in suspended animation and will not require anything, including food, water, or bathroom breaks. But their minds will understand that they are in a prison. And the mind is the part that will eventually change. Once it does, you can decide if, and when, you want to release them back to their world."

"So I won't be dragging them off somewhere?" asked Peter, trying to embrace this new concept.

"It wouldn't be practical to have a bunch of wriggling children hanging on your horse, would it? However, people will believe that is exactly what you did. But in truth, they will have never left their physical place, but only be held in a temporal portal that you created."

"A what?" Peter was now thoroughly confused.

"A portal is a place where you will suspend time. It will be invisible to others, but you will be able to see and visit it whenever you want. The children will be able to see what is going on around them, but be unable to interact with anyone outside their portal. This will hopefully cause their rehabilitation into a more productive societal use."

"You do know I am a simple chimney sweep, and all this is greatly above my understanding?" Peter said.

"This will all become clear to you at some point. You need not grasp everything I am telling you right now. But make no mistake, you must learn and be able to do these things or you will not be able to perform your duties."

For the rest of his day, he worked with Aeon in focusing the time continuum into ever smaller circles. Aeon showed Peter that one could freeze two different areas and actually move the one into the other. He explained this is how Peter would eventually trap his prisoners.

"What is interesting," he told Peter, "is that Santa

actually discovered this part by accident. He uses this concept to be more efficient in delivering his gifts to the world. He has no idea of the other uses it can be used for, and you are never to let him know."

"I am not sure I could tell him anything as I, myself, am not too certain what I am doing," said Peter.

"That is only true for today. Tomorrow will be another story."

Pierre's
Caberet

CHAPTER ELEVEN

After months of training and learning, Peter felt he was as prepared as he might ever be. Santa had come to visit his assistant toward the end of November to see if he was ready. As Santa and Peter were discussing how and where they would begin the journey for that special night, a young Moor elf came up to them. When they looked down at him, he said, "I want to help you both and I'd like to go with you!"

Santa looked at the young boy, and with a chuckle in his voice said, "And you are?"

The young boy said, "I am Peter, too. Only my name is Boutros, because I was born in Egypt. That means 'Peter' in Arabic."

"Doesn't that make you Muslim? How is it you believe in Christianity?" asked Santa.

"I was named after the three Pope Peters. I was raised, Christian. But if I wasn't, I believe in you and what you are doing for everyone. You are the great Gift-giver and this is your assistant. I can be his assistant, and I want to help you distribute gifts or punishments. I want to come with you on your trip."

Peter said, "That is very kind of you Boutros, but as this is my first time doing this, I am not sure yet if I need an assistant, myself. Of course, it is up to Santa."

Santa said, "Let's wait for this particular trip out this year, Boutros. You may ask me next year, and I will see how we are fairing. Right now I need to train Peter on his job, and cannot take on another assistant. But I thank you for the offering."

The little black elf tried arguing with the two men without success. He felt dejected as he knew he could be a good helper to the two gift givers, if they gave him a chance. He was not going to let this pass quietly. He planned to be around far more often from now on until they gave in. But today was not the day, as they were already preparing to leave.

Once Boutros finally left, Santa returned back to Peter and said, "Now we will disembark by boat in Spain. Amerigo and Avalanche will be waiting for us there. We will begin in Spain and Portugal and move north into France, Germany, Poland and then swing back do to England. After that, we work our way north and east into the Netherlands, and then head south to cover Czechoslovakia, Lichtenstein, Austria, and Italy."

"That's an awful lot of miles. Except for Germany, I have never been to any of those countries. Maybe we should get Boutros back here."

Santa laughed, "This is a piece of cake compared to Christmas Eve. You sure you wouldn't like to join me for that?"

Peter held up his hand and shaking his head said, "No thank you. I think this is all I will ever wish to take on. When do we get the final flight plans from Sky?"

Santa smiled, "I'll let you go visit her and get them for us. I get to see enough of her for the Christmas Eve visit a couple weeks after this. How are you two getting along?"

Peter turned red at the question but kept a serious face, "We are getting along fine, thank you."

Santa knew there was more to his answer than Peter let on, but said no more.

Peter asked, "How will our horses get to Europe before us?"

"The network we have set up. We have a good number of elves in different countries with areas set up for my gifts and your switches. This way we don't have to take everything at once, which would be too cumbersome, if not impossible."

"We have a network? Do other elves live down there by choice?" Peter seemed concerned for them.

"Quite so. The elves will often trade off from year to year, but many are quite satisfied living in the south. Not everyone has had to deal with the type of treatment you and other elves received, I am thankful to say. There are talls who are kind and are respectful of others. You just haven't had the chance to meet them. But you will soon."

"Well, that will come as quite a surprise if and when I do. Especially when you consider the role I am playing and my physical features."

"Oh, and speaking of physical features, that reminds me, Ulzana Stichinsew is waiting to make you whatever outfit you would like to wear for this position. As you already know, I wear the long robe of my ancestor, with the priestly garments beneath, and the tall miter hat. Have you given thought to what you would like to wear?"

"I prefer a simple brown robe with a long hood," replied Peter.

"Why so ordinary? I was thinking something in gold with piping down the front and maybe a bishop's cap." Santa said.

"A simple brown robe with a long hood to hide my features would be enough. I will not be viewed as a happy character in future history. I think the less colorful I am, the less attention I will draw to myself. I do not need, nor do I ask, for more than that."

Peter said the last part with finality. Santa shrugged and said, "As you wish. Ulzana will make it as you ask but do go see her soon, so she can get your measurements. She is already

working on several outfits for different elves for the upcoming
Christmas holiday."

"I will see her tomorrow," Peter promised.

Peter said goodbye to Santa and headed for Sky's home.
He knocked on her door. She told him to come on in. He found
her pouring over charts for their journey for the Eve of the
Feast of St. Nicholas. Once again, as always, he was taken by
her looks, as she was intensely frowning at the maps before her.

"Bad news?" he asked looking at her furrowed brow.

"No, not really," she said suddenly brightening, "I was
just tracking a minor cell coming off the Atlantic that could
bring you quite a bit of snow in Norway. Actually, the rest of
Europe looks exceedingly favorable for your trip."

She showed him the wind currents coming up from the
South and said, "It actually may be quite warm for this time
of year. Except for Norway and Sweden, you may have
exceptionally good weather."

They were standing quite close as they had done in
during previous meetings. Often when she was teaching him
how to read weather and climate charts. He had wanted to ask
all the other times and finally got up the courage to do so.

"How is it that you can stand to be so close to me? Don't
my features repulse you?"

Sky looked shocked, "Why would you think that? Have I
ever said, or done, anything to make you think that?"

"Absolutely not. I guess that is why I am curious."

"Physical features aren't important to me. It is the inner
you that is important, and I find that person most attractive.
You are a kindhearted and intelligent person, which is far more
important than your looks. I have always enjoyed the time we
have spent together."

Peter would have prayed for such an answer, however,

upon actually hearing it, he now did not know how to respond to it. He came up with the only thought he could and asked, "Would you be willing to go out to dinner with me sometime?"

Sky started giggling, "Of course, silly! Anytime you would like."

Peter felt he might leap right out of his skin. "Could you tonight?"

"If you would like."

"How about I swing by and pick you up at 6:30?" he asked.

"I could meet you somewhere, to save the extra walk if you'd rather," she offered

"Actually I'd like to show you something, so I'd rather come here."

"As you wish, I'll be ready," she smiled sweetly, "Now can we finish up this briefing on your upcoming trip?"

Peter knew he would not be able to concentrate, but agreed to her request. He tried his hardest to pay attention to what she was showing him, but mostly only nodded and grunted at her pointing and explaining the movements of the jet streams. It would be a long time until 6:30, and he suddenly felt the need for a bath.

After he finished reviewing Sky's information he stepped out her door and practiced what he wanted to demonstrate to her that night.

He arrived at his home and jumped in the bath. After he toweled off he was able to comb his normally wild hair flat against his head. He then shaved but was so nervous he nicked his face in a few places. He stopped the bleeding and had the paper on his face when he dressed. He ran out at 6:15 and practically skipped to Sky's house.

When he arrived he was astounded at how pretty she

looked. She had replaced her normal look of loose pants and a smock with a lovely dress that fell to just above her shoes. The cut of her dress accentuated her attractive figure, which could only be guessed at ordinarily. He stammered for a second before he commented on how nice she looked.

She giggled again and removed the pieces of paper from the nicked areas of his face. He instantly blushed red and apologized. She sloughed it off and said, "You know, you might look handsome in a beard. Have you ever considered it?"

Peter said he hadn't before, but immediately thought he might try to grow one for her.

Then Sky asked, "So where are we off to?"

He smiled and said, "I will have to show you," and moved in close to her.

He placed his hands on her waist and said, "Ready?"

She nodded, and then Peter stopped and moved through time until they stood before the restaurant he had planned. All of this happened in the blink of an eye. He then released the continuum.

"That's amazing!" Sky said almost breathlessly, "I had always known about the time continuum and had watched Santa use it a couple times, but I never actually participated in a time and space movement. How exciting!"

He was pleased with her reaction and then opened the door for his date. This was going to be the best evening of his life.

They sat and talked about many things, mostly about each other's past and about Peter's new role at the North Pole. They shared a delicious dinner and some hot chocolate. When they were finished, she asked if they could return the way they had come. And although it took the briefest of moments, Peter managed to steal his first kiss ever during the short span.

CHAPTER TWELVE

The day had arrived and Peter stood next to Santa in his long brown robe with his face covered in dark stubble. They were accompanied by Annie, Sky, Forrest and a few other well-wishers. Santa and Peter kissed their ladies goodbye and boarded the flying boat as Santa called it. Willie Movinmuch, the elves principal transportation specialist, fired up the engine.

Santa had explained that they could not land where people would see the flying boat, as most people were still trying to get used to seeing a flying horse. He told Peter how he had heard people yell the word "witchcraft" on more than one occasion over that, and he could only imagine how they would react to the sight of a craft such as this.

They landed in the water about a mile offshore where their boat was waiting to take them the rest of the way to shore. As they moved toward the shore they could see a large crowd that had gathered to greet the famous St. Nicholas. Santa had done this trip for decades and every year more and more people turned out to see the great Gift-giver arrive in Spain.

Upon approaching the audience Santa held up his hands and the scepter he carried. When they were quieted, he said to them, "This is my assistant, Peter Black, I have entrusted him to advise me of the naughty children in your villages. To the young ones that he deems unfit to receive my gifts, he will leave birch branches behind for them. You know what to do with those branches." To this, the crowd laughed. "I trust Peter Black's judgment completely, and you should, also. Children need to be taught to lead good lives, and it is up to you to instruct them. Those who do not pay heed to his warnings could have dire consequences going forward."

The crowd mumbled to each other as to what the consequences could be, but St. Nicholas explained no further. Then the two horses were led to St. Nicholas and the stranger in the long cloak. They mounted their horses and the procession began through the streets. As soon as the crowd had dwindled the two gift-givers went to work and began leaving their goods for the children.

It wasn't until the third village before Peter needed to leave the first of the branches. He knew of two children that were not well behaved at all. One of the children he saw stole things from other children, and occasionally from adults as well. The other he knew had bitten other children numerous times.

After that, there were several switches that Peter left for a variety of crimes. Lying to both children and adults, stealing, harming others and often animals, destroying another person's property, and so on.

He got to one child's house and looked into his heart. He was sickened by what he saw and woke the child.

The child was startled to find a dark person in a dark cloak and started to yell out. But Peter had already invoked the time continuum so that the scream would not be heard by anyone except the two of them. When the boy quieted, Peter asked the child, "Is what I see true? Have you started three different fires at other people's houses?"

The boy's eyes went wide and he stared at the dark man for a long time before answering. He finally said, "You don't know that. And you cannot prove it. Now get out before I scream again. It is none of your business what I do, or what I did, now GET OUT!"

Peter shook his head and said, "You caused the death of

two other children and an old woman. You can scream all you wish because no one will hear you. If you are not sorry for your actions you shall leave me no choice."

The boy started screaming again and Peter opened a portal before the boy. He pushed the boy through the opening. The boy was captured as if in a one way looking glass peering out. When he finally stopped yelling, Peter said to the boy, "Here you are and here you will stay until you have reformed and are penitent for your sins. You will not grow older, but time shall pass nonetheless, and all those shall grow older around you. Once you have atoned for your crimes, I shall come to release you. You will not be hungry or thirsty while you are in my prism, but you will feel no joy or happiness, either. Reflect on the misery you have caused others and be contrite in your sorrow."

With that Peter Black had imprisoned his first child. When his parents woke the next day, all they knew was their boy was gone. Whether they were distraught or overjoyed over this fact, did not matter. He would not be seen for at least a year.

In other villages, children began disappearing. Most of these children were known troublemakers, and although no one would say so outwardly, often few were missed and almost nobody ever went looking for them, not even their own family.

It did not take long for the rumors to begin spreading about the stranger that accompanied St. Nicholas on the eve of his holiday. As the two rode and flew through Europe the stories flew with them. Children began to fear the figure of "Black Peter" as he was now called throughout the countryside.

Of course, he was called different names in different places. He was known as Zwarte Piet in the Netherlands, Pere

Fouettard in France, Schmutzli in Switzerland, Knecht Ruprecht in Germany along with, Hanstrapp or Rupelz in the French region of Alsace, Pelzebock or Pelznickel in Northwest, Hans Muff in Rhineland, Bartel or the Wild Bear in Silesia, Gumphinkel with a bear in Hesse, Buttenmandl in Bavaria, or Black Pit close to the Dutch border. In the Palatinate, both Nicholas and his attendant were sometimes known as Stappklos. And with each name he was given, he was given a different description along with it.

It was frequently said that he was the servant of St. Nicholas, and often his slave. There were stories that Peter had done unspeakable crimes, and that he had been enslaved by the good bishop to serve as punishment for his past deeds.

Both Santa and Peter shook their heads over this. They knew the fear that Peter now generated. And the threats of his arrival were almost enough to dissuade the most misbehaved child into better behavior.

By now Peter sported a full thick beard that rivaled Santa's. As Sky guessed, it softened his features greatly and made him easier on the eyes. Another part of the confusion about the look of Zwarte Piet was due to Boutros. He kept his promise and tormented both Santa and Peter, separately and together until they finally gave way.

Moreover, Peter was nondescript in his robes, Boutros instead wore brightly colored outfits looking more like a court jester from an earlier age. On this particular day, he wore a royal purple outfit with a purple cape to match and bright gold and white billowed breeches with tights. He finished the outfit with a purple hat adorned with a long gold feather.

Boutros would ride with Santa in Norway, Finland, and Sweden helping dispense gifts and switches where told. Boutros would ride in Santa' time continuum but was never taught how to use it on his own. Although Peter would ride along with Santa and Boutros, he allowed Boutros to administer the switches, while he imprisoned any children that required punishment, which was now becoming rare indeed.

In the meantime, the romance between Sky and Peter blossomed and on December 3, 1789, just a couple days before that year's journey, the couple was married.

The ceremony took place at the chapel at the foot of Elf Mountain. Pastor Goinpeace spoke about the love the couple had for each other and the love that was given them by all the elves of the North Pole.

Denny Sweetooth told Hilda she had to sit this banquet out as the mother of the groom was not going to work on this so long as he and Pierre were in residence at the North Pole. Though the rush of the Eve of St. Nick and Christmas were well and truly in high gear, everyone attended that could, making it one of the largest events since the welcome banquet of Santa and Mrs. Claus.

Speaking of this, Peter had the best of all best men, which was Kristopher Nicholas Kringle. Not to be outdone, Sky had the CEO of the entire North Pole, Ann Marie Kringle. The Clauses were as proud as any parents could be and spoke eloquently of their two friends at the reception. Hilda cried and cried with joy, never believing in their past life that this day would ever come.

Peter promised his new bride that upon his return, they would take an extensive honeymoon. When Peter came back from their journey that year, he let her choose wherever she wished to go. Sky kept her wishes to a minimum, asking instead for a newer home for her and her new husband. Her request was granted and a new home was built for the couple. He was now closer to Santa and Annie's home in the

Woodlands, and his old home is where Hilda stayed by her own choice. The new residence was larger than Sky's former house, and the elves placed a good many special touches in the new home. After all, nothing was too good for Santa's Assistant and his new bride.

Life couldn't have been much better for Peter and he was grateful for all he had. And even as he was cursed by many in Europe for doing his job, he was as happy as he thought he might ever be. For many years they were an extremely happy couple and Peter enjoyed his annual visits with Santa and Boutros.

Of course, that is when God will often put you to the test. And that happened shortly after the new century came to pass.

CHAPTER THIRTEEN

Peter had captured many children and had imprisoned them in his special fortress. He had religiously checked on each one every year. Many of them he had set free. So long as he could see true remorse in their hearts and their realization that they had done terrible wrongs.

Some he knew he had kept for an exceptionally long time. Of course, the ones he released fed the stories of Black Peter and how he took the children to his lair and kept them there, especially as no one could see them around their home.

But a new figure was cropping up in the legends about Peter. And this monster truly was one. Peter kept seeing drawings of a being that was called Krampus. But this was one of the names that Peter had been called for years. However, this Krampus was now being depicted as a beast with one cloven foot, great long black fur, an elongated bright red tongue with eyes to match, and long fangs. Atop his head were the long curled horns of a goat.

Peter wasn't amused with this new look, and he wondered where it had come from and why. Further, he was now accused of taking children over the last many years that he knew he hadn't imprisoned. Although many of these children were admittedly of poor behavior, Peter either had not thought their actions warranted his severe punishment, or he hadn't met the same children he was accused of taking.

He finally met his nemesis in the beginning of the new century. During his 1901 visit, he came to a house where he stood face to face with the creature in the drawings. He invoked the time continuum to freeze the monster, but it was unaffected, though all around them time was frozen.

"Who and what are you?" Peter asked the being before

him.

"I am Krampus," the creature snarled.

"No, that is my name, you have only stolen it. And apparently, you have terrorized many families and have stolen several children using it!"

"I do as my master tells me to do. Just as you do what that fat red elf tells you to do." The creature howled at his own insult of Santa.

"And just who is your master?" asked Peter.

"Like you, he goes by many names, Beelzebub, Abaddon, the King of Babylon, Lucifer, and Satan to name but a few."

Peter was shocked but did his best not to let it show. He had held a suspicion looking at the many pictures of this creature, but never spoke it aloud. He needed to know the true name of the demon before him and asked again, "And which of his minions are you?"

"I am who I am, and you need not know more," answered the demon.

"And how am I to know my adversary if I do not recognize his name?"

"I am not your adversary you puny little elf. You are a pretender of something more important than you ever hope to be. You are a miserable worm pretending to be important. And you are not to interfere with my work for my Master." the creature spewed this along with a string of obscenities.

Peter saw the young boy squirming and crying in the demon's claws and asked, "Why are you taking children? And where are you taking them? What use could your master have for them?"

The demon dropped the young boy and snarled at Peter. The boy crawled into a corner of his room and curled into a ball.

"My Master's business is His own. These children serve Him, as I serve Him. You, the great pretender, are not to interfere, especially with his favored son on earth!" The fowl being realized he spoke of something he shouldn't have, and howled again, this time as if stabbed.

Peter knew he just learned something of great import. He could not imagine who he was referring to but now knew the most unclean had a favorite who was already here on earth. How could he recognize him, and what would he do if he found him? Would he dare incur Satan's wrath by enslaving his favorite human? And in the meantime, how could he stop this demon from snatching more children like this one? Was he going to take this boy again, or did he forget him? How could Peter stop this being from making Peter's own name more hated than it already was?

Peter sensed he was out-gunned in this encounter and knew he would have to get help before he could do or say much more. He said, "We shall meet again, and next time it will not be so pleasant for you."

The demon howled once again, this time sounding spiteful and including another stream of obscenities said to Peter, "You can do nothing, and you are nothing! I shall do as I please, and you cannot stop me. If you try, I will tear you apart and leave your master, and your God, one dead elf. My master will be served, and yours will fall!"

The demon leaped through the open door and out of the house where they stood. Peter realized that time had begun again and wondered who had frozen whom. The boy scrambled under his covers and was crying softly under his sheet.

Peter realized he was shaking from the encounter. He had difficulty finishing his rounds that night. He would look at the children and could see nothing about their personalities, not knowing if they were good or bad. Santa was several towns behind him. They were heading to Norway and the Netherlands next. He decided to head back and tell Santa to let Boutros do the rounds there by himself.

When he caught up with Santa, Santa could see that Peter was shaking and asked what happened.

"I had an encounter with the Devil's servant who has been stealing children. I am having trouble completing my duties tonight. We will need to have a serious meeting concerning this upon our return."

Santa nodded his head and said, "You return at once. Boutros and I will complete tonight's deliveries. Think about who else we should involve with this, but say nothing to anyone until we have had time to assess the situation. You are fortunate to be in one piece after this encounter. We best not have a second until we know what we can do."

Peter told Santa of the demon's threats, and Santa again urged him to return to the North Pole immediately. Peter turned Avalanche around and flew off to the Northwest as instructed. He was already thinking of who from the village needed to be brought into their meeting.

CHAPTER FOURTEEN

Peter told Sky about the brush with Satan's servant. She was extremely distraught that some "thing" had threatened her husband. He pleaded with her to keep quiet and keep their secret, at least until they knew how to proceed. The next day, instead of Santa resting all day as he normally did after his Eve of the Feast of St. Nicholas journey, he sent a message to Peter to meet with him and Aeon at his home.

Santa invited Reverend Cyril Goinpeace to join them, as he was an ecumenical scholar and would help shed light on what they were up against. He and Peter showed up at the same time. In her official capacity as CEO of the North Pole, Annie also attended the meeting, more to keep an eye on her exhausted husband. She made everyone comfortable with cakes and various bread, along with coffee and cocoa.

The meeting began with Peter describing as best he could the physical characteristics of the demon he encountered. He talked about the drawings he had seen before and then said, "He was close to six feet, not including his horns which added another two feet. He was covered head to hoof in long, black fur. As I told Santa, he had red eyes, a long red tongue which he kept flicking after he spoke. His hands were long and slender claws. His lower legs were more like a goat's and ended in a cloven hoof and a foot resembling a claw. The horns went straight up but curved as they did.

Aeon produced a picture from a binder he was carrying similar to the drawings Peter had seen before, "Did it look like this?" and showed Peter the drawing.

"Yes, that's it." Peter nodded.

"Well, that explains that," said Aeon, "I always wondered how Peter could go from looking like either Knecht

Ruprecht or Boutros to that hideous creature. I guess now I do."

Santa looked at the drawing and then the Reverend and asked, "Pastor have you any ideas on this beast? Can you shed any light on who it is? Why is it coming on my ancestors holiday, and most importantly how do we stop it?"

Cyril shook his head and said, "It could be any number of Satan's demons. The three that immediately come to mind are; Abdiel, the lord of slaves, Ahaza, the seizing demon of the night, or possibly Alu, another night demon. These mostly because it is taking children. But it could be any one of a hundred others. Most of his Legion have never been identified or viewed by mortal man."

"As far as why it is appearing in our world, they have been here long before and during the time of Christ. In fact, in the Bible according to Mark, we read where Jesus casts out a demon. In Mark's account, a demon had possessed a man's son.

"This demon caused epileptic-like seizures, in which the son was at times thrown down to wallow on the ground, made to foam at the mouth and could not speak. Jesus' own disciples were unable to cast this demon out. Finally, Christ came and rebuked the unclean spirit: 'Deaf and dumb spirit, I command you, come out of him and enter him no more'. Apparently, Christ was not speaking to the person, but to the demon in possession of him."

Peter said, "He threatened me. He told me he would 'tear me apart'. Can he do that?"

"I am not certain about a demon killing you, though we know it can possess a person. Now in Job, we know that God exercises power over the devil, telling Satan he may test Job, but not to take Job's life. However, God did not prevent Satan to take the life of Job's family members. So we know the devil has the power to kill humans, should God allow it. We might assume that his demons have a similar power if granted by the devil or Him."

"Great," said Peter, "I might get killed by one of Satan's demons. That is if the villagers don't get to me first thinking I am the monster in the drawings."

Cyril looking now at the drawing said, "I doubt the townsfolk would mistake you for this monster. You do not look anything like the creature in this drawing."

Annie waved her hands and said, "Now let's not get carried away. Nobody or nothing is going to kill you, Peter."

Aeon said, "I agree, there is nothing to suggest that you are taken out by Krampus."

"I AM Krampus!" yelled Peter.

"Sorry, you know what I meant," Aeon corrected himself.

"So what am I supposed to do?" asked a frustrated Peter.

"Do nothing," said Aeon, "This monster has been running around for several years now. This is the first time you have stumbled into it. Just try avoiding it in the future."

Santa nodded his head in agreement, "Continue to do your task as you are able, but avoid this demon if you can. I would not do anything to provoke it. We are powerless to prevent it from taking the children it, or the devil, wants anyway."

"I hate to see the devil get its way in any scenario," said Cyril, "But I must agree. We need to allow God to deal with this, as He is the only being strong enough to do so. However, to protect yourself, I advise that you carry a vial of holy water in case you run into him by accident."

"Do you think that could help?" asked Peter.

"It couldn't hurt," answered Cyril, "And it may chase it

off."

"Do you think it might kill it?"

Aeon said, "I don't think you can kill something that is not of this earth in the first place. If it is a demon as we suspect, it is probably one of the fallen angels that joined Lucifer from the beginning."

"I quite agree with Aeon," said Cyril, "For instance in the Bible, we know Daniel prayed for Godly understanding as to the events of Israel in the Latter Days. The same day Daniel prayed, God instructed one of His angels to go to Daniel and deliver His answer. The angel immediately left heaven for earth, a journey that takes but a moment of thought. Instead, it took three weeks for the angel to get to Daniel. The angel explained that he had been held up by a demonic being whom the angel referred to as 'The Prince of the Kingdom of Persia'. In other words, this angel had been attacked by a powerful demon, the demon assigned to influence the king of Persia at the time. This angel could not defeat this powerful demonic being on his own strength, so he had to call on Michael, the angel whom God had assigned to protect Israel. Thus, we see that some demonic beings are more powerful than some angelic beings."

"You DO know you are not making me feel any better about all this, right?" said Peter sourly.

Cyril preached, "As the Apostle Paul instructs: 'Therefore take up the whole armor of God, that you may be able to withstand in the evil day, and having done all, to stand. Stand therefore, having girded your waist with truth, having put on the breastplate of righteousness, and having shod your feet with the preparation of the gospel of peace; above all, taking the shield of faith with which you will be able to quench all the fiery darts of the wicked one.'"

"Rather than going in for the battle, I suggest as we have already said, you stay clear of it. Don't give it any more reason to torment you," Annie said hoping to end the discussion.

"One question," said Peter, "What about the naughty children? Do I continue my rounds up there, or just avoid these countries altogether?"

Everyone looked at Santa for his answer. He thought for a moment and then said, "I will need time to contemplate this and come up with a solution, providing there is one. Let me ask this, how many children have you imprisoned in the countries this demon is visiting?"

"Throughout the Alpine region and Northern Germany where he stalks, most likely less than one hundred," replied Peter.

"You will have to visit them all at least, and whether or not they have been rehabilitated you will probably need to release them."

Peter stared at Santa and then gasped a long sigh.

"I think we all need to think about this for some time," Annie said as she moved to the door, "If any of you come up with another idea, please feel free to visit us immediately."

Everyone knew the meeting was over. Annie was anxious for her husband to get some rest before he tended to Christmas Eve details. She thanked them all for coming and assured them that clearer heads and answers would prevail at a later date.

CHAPTER FIFTEEN

From the moment he left the meeting, Peter knew he could not give up without a fight. He said as much to Aeon and Cyril as they left the Clauses. He asked the reverend to please see if there was something his ecumenical council might know, or if there was something through the teachings and his wealth of books that might help.

So many children. And he was certain that all the children taken were not deserving of their fate. But if they were, Peter might trap them in time, but he did not take them to Hell where these children were now. The very thought made him sick with sadness and grief. But how does one fight Satan's demon and live to talk about it?

Several weeks after the Christmas holidays were over, Peter received a knock on his door. He welcomed Reverend Goinpeace into his house. Cyril said he met someone who knew more about demons and how to cast them back down where they belonged. He asked Peter to accompany him to his chapel.

For the first time since meeting his monster, Peter thought there might be a glimmer of hope. If this man knew anything at all about defeating demons, Peter would try putting it into practice.

As they walked to the chapel Peter tried asking Cyril about the stranger. Cyril said little to nothing and just kept saying, 'You'll see.' The reverend opened the door for him. Peter walked in and saw a black hooded and robed figure up near and facing the altar. Peter wasn't sure if he should interrupt the man as he might be praying.

Cyril took his elbow and walked him toward the front of the chapel. The person turned and faced them and removed the black hood.

She was lovely with silver-gold hair and a long slender face with blue-green shimmering eyes. At first, Peter thought a joke was being played on him. When she spoke, her voice was firm but musical. She said, "Do not let my appearance deceive you. Many from the dark side made that mistake and it cost them dearly. You have a demon problem, and I am your solution. My name is Gavenrael Devereaux."

"A beautiful name for a beautiful lady to be sure. I am curious as to how is it you know about demons?" Peter asked carefully.

"I have faced them before in many countries and many forms. Only one had taken a physical form before, most were through possessions, and a few of those contained many demons in each person."

"Truly?" Peter said with surprise.

"Yes. Tell me about yours." Gavenrael's eyes softened, "I can see in your face he has haunted you for a time now."

Cyril said he had other duties to attend to and excused himself from Peter and Gavenrael. He left through the front of the chapel.

Peter had the drawing Aeon had given him of the demon, and as she looked at it, he told her of the discourse they had last season. He explained to her he had been out there for quite some years, but Peter had not run into him until this last year. He also told her of both his and the demon's abilities to stop and hold time, and Peter's efforts to imprison the truly terrible boys and girls who harm others. He told her how this demon seemed to take children at his, or his master's, whim. He said he was not sure of their fate and he guessed they had not been seen again.

He found himself getting highly emotional explaining

this demon and heard his own voice getting higher in pitch and volume.

Gavenrael reached over to Peter and touched his shoulder. Peter instantly calmed down and began breathing slower.

"That is amazing! How did you do that?" he said in a calmer demeanor.

She smiled at Peter, "I will teach you later. Now besides verbally threatening you, did it try to do anything physical to you?"

"No. It actually kept a pretty good distance from me, which I was thankful for."

"That means he was afraid of you, and that his threats were empty at best," said Gavenrael.

"Wait. It was afraid of me? It was me who was scared out of my mind! This was an insidious monster!"

Gavenrael smiled again. "There are two things you need to learn right now. The first is that demons hate to fight for their prey. They can and will do anything when invited in, but they are cowards at heart and will avoid confrontation if they can. Tell me, when you met him did he take a child in your presence?"

Peter shook his head, "He had one in his grip, but he seemed to lose interest when he spoke to me."

"That's because he figured you would challenge him for the child and he wasn't interested in a fight. The second thing you need to know is demons do not get to wander free at full force in our world. If they did, they would have destroyed and corrupted everything by now. Instead, they only have a temporary power that can be used here. Unless they find a way to gather more."

Gavenrael continued, "Think of it like flying or

swimming. You can fly around, or I can dive into the water and hold my breath for a while. But after a time you run out of strength and have to land if flying, and I run out of air if swimming. So we both would need to come back to our own land. This is also true of demons. They can only come into our world for a time, but can't stay for long.

"This is why you only ran into him in certain countries and on a certain date. Now a demon can take longer stays on our plane of existence if they have a way of doing so, like getting help from people."

"Why would anyone in their right mind help keep a demon around?" Peter asked.

"Most people do so without knowing it. We can't help ourselves. In my swimming example, the 'air' that demons need to stay longer in our world is energy. Spiritual energy is the strongest energy on earth. Evil spirits need dark or negative energy and positive spirits need light or positive energy. If you can starve a demon of negative energy, you suffocate him from this world, just like a swimmer with no air. I suspect that he was afraid of you because you possess a great deal of positive energy."

"I sure wasn't feeling too positive about it when I was near it," Peter said.

"Nonetheless, he knew you had light energy and he probably fled from you before he lost too much power. Now the trick is to increase that positive vibration as you stand before him. We will be working on that going forward."

Peter looked surprised and asked, "Are you planning to teach me to deal with this thing?"

Gavenrael smiled and said, "That, and I intend to go with you on the next Eve of St. Nicholas and fight with you."

"Really? You think you can take this monster on and

defeat it?"

"Not me, we. I am convinced that if you are properly trained, between the two of us we can teach this devil servant a lesson he would not soon forget," she said.

"Where and when do we start?" Peter asked.

"Right now, if you'd like," Gavenrael said smiling.

Peter nodded enthusiastically.

"Okay, the first thing we need to work on is your aura and your confidence. As I told you earlier, you are stronger than the demon. Which we need to give him a name since that will give you more power over it."

"Reverend Goinpeace said it could be a demon named Ahazu. Could we call it that?" asked Peter.

"We need to be careful not to call the demon by his wrong name. It could have a backfire effect. We don't want to give more power into the wrong hands. What do the villagers call it?"

"They call it Krampus, but that is one of my names," complained Peter.

"Better to call him by a name that he knows, then to call him a wrong demon's name. Besides, don't you go by many names?" asked Gavenrael.

"I guess."

"If the villagers have begun calling this half beast by that name, you might be better off to let it go, as it may never be yours again. Or at least the name Krampus would have different faces going forward."

"Very well, Krampus it is," said Peter in a resigned tone.

"Okay, so we run into Krampus, what do we do first?" asked Gavenrael.

"Scream?"

"I am being serious. What is the first thing your heart

tells you to do?"

"Pray it doesn't kill us." Peter was being serious now.

"Actually, you are right. We want to pray in a low breath to ourselves and meditate only good and happy thoughts as we do this. This will bring more positive energy into the room. This will eventually starve out the negative energy and therefore the demon of his power to remain here."

"You keep saying 'him' and 'his', how do you know it is a him?" asked Peter.

Gavenrael shrugged, "We normally refer to all deities in the masculine. God, the devil, demons, are all referred to as male, whether right or wrong. Besides, again making it seem more like a man strips him of more power. Wouldn't you rather take on a simple man than a beast?"

"This wasn't a 'simple man'," said Peter.

"And neither are you. Remember, he was more afraid of you than you were of him."

"You keep saying that. Reverend Goinpeace said the demon could kill me if it, or rather he, wanted," said Peter nervously.

"Actually it could not unless it had permission from its master, and its master probably wouldn't want to incur God's wrath by giving that permission. Especially if Satan had nothing to gain from it."

"How do you mean?"

"When you eventually leave this earth are you expecting to go to heaven or hell?" asked Gavenrael.

"Heaven, of course."

"So Satan would never get you, so why kill you? He would gain nothing, and might lose much in the bargain."

Peter hadn't thought of this before and it instantly made him feel stronger. It also made perfect sense. "Okay, so I quit worrying about my life, now how do I stop him from stealing others?"

"You already did," smiled Gavenrael.

"I don't know that I had anything to do with that."

"What did I say the first lesson about demons was?"

"Demons hate to fight for their prey," recited Peter.

"Correct, the mere fact that you showed up at that time and place convinced Krampus to release the child. Every time you appear in front of him, that will be the case. Especially if you command him to do so. But before we delve into that, we need to teach you how to be prepared and centered."

Gavenrael moved to Peter and had him sit in a chair. She placed her hands on either side of his head. "Now, just breathe deeply. Breathe in through your nose and release the breath slowly out through your mouth."

He did as she asked and she had him do this several times. Once she heard his breathing become deeper and calmer she said, "Good. Now think of a happy memory, something that brings you great joy. It can be real or imagined, but you have to be able to visualize it completely."

"Oh, it is quite real," Peter said as he remembered his wedding day and the way Sky looked at him as they said their vows. It filled Peter with a bright aura.

"Excellent!" Gavenrael could feel the lightness throughout the room, "Krampus wouldn't stand a chance against this, with or without me."

"But you will be there, right?" asked Peter.

"You have my promise. Now we need to teach you so we can count on you being able to produce this lightness on demand and under stressful circumstances."

"Like when we're in the room with it, I mean him."

"Yes. Now let's begin teaching you control over your

spirit."

The two worked for the next three hours on different spiritual and physical exercises to strengthen Peter's resolve and energy until he had nothing left. He didn't have the power to use the continuum to take him home and could only trudge slowly through the village. He told Sky about what had happened and went to bed and slept into the next day.

CHAPTER SIXTEEN

They trained for the next several months. Gavenrael worked continuously on strengthening his spirit and teaching him to control his mind and thoughts. She showed him how to read other auras around him and to pick up on negative feelings or energy.

She showed him how to deflect negative waves with his own positive vibrations. She explained that this would be more difficult when he encountered Krampus, but that if Peter practiced enough, he could face a room full of demons and not be overcome.

After a time, Peter asked if any type of physical protection or weaponry existed that he could use against Krampus.

Gavenrael said she had been waiting, but thought that now might be as good a time as any. She went to the back of the chapel and returned moments later with a small wooden box.

The first items she pulled out were three small vials, each a different color.

"Let me guess, holy water?" asked Peter.

"Not just any holy water. This first vial in the red tube is from the resting place of the first St. Nicholas, who, as you may already know, is buried at the Jerpoint Abbey, County Kilkenny in Ireland. This second green vial is from Down Cathedral, in the Cathedral Church of the Holy and Undivided Trinity in Ireland, which is the resting place of St. Patrick. This third and most important vial is clear and contains holy water from the Church of the Holy Sepulcher in the City of Jerusalem, which is the burial tomb of Jesus Christ. This holy water is the most powerful on earth and is only to be used in an extreme emergency, as it is not easily replaced

"Wow, okay, I got it."

She next produced another small bottle. She said, "This is red oil, which is exceptional at disrupting the demon's negative energy and demonic obsession or possession. Before you run into Krampus, place a drop on your forehead to disrupt a possession. Then place a drop on the back of your neck to prevent demonic obsession."

"I have heard of possession, but what is an obsession?" asked Peter.

"It is obsession when the demon acts externally against the person whom it besets, and possession when it acts internally." answered Gavenrael.

"So I need only put it on the back of my neck?" asked Peter.

"Do both to be sure. Krampus may attempt to possess you if he thinks you're too strong externally. We don't want to take any chances. Plus, he might bring other demons with him to accomplish that very act. After all, we know he is aware of your existence and he might also be preparing a little welcome committee for your next meeting."

Peter shifted uncomfortably at the thought of this. "Is this as rare as the holy waters?"

"Not at all. I made that batch up myself. It is a simple combination of St. John's Wort flowers and olive oil, fermented until it turns red and then placed in a clear container. You can douse yourself in it if you wish. Just make sure you get your forehead and the back of your neck." Gavenrael said.

She then pulled a canvas pouch from the box. "This is salt. You can use this to purify a spot. Say Krampus is after a child but hasn't gotten to them yet. If you sprinkle this around the child he won't be able to take the child."

"Is this salt from somewhere special?" asked Peter.

Gavenrael laughed, "Actually it is Kosher salt. I find it works quite well."

She replaced the pouch in the box and said, "Now I understand you go for simple garb and choose to wear but a nondescript robe and hood?"

"Just as you do. For me, it is a habit from going in and out of chimneys. I used to wear next to nothing as I cleaned them. I find the robe cumbersome at times, but it helps keep me warm in December."

"I am going to ask you to wear something more," she said. "This is extremely powerful, and will help your spirit, which we already know will be your best defense."

She pulled out two linen squares with pictures on them and connected with a brown piece of leather.

"This is a brown scapular. Called 'Our Lady of Mount Carmel,' it is a sacramental piece associated with promises of Mary's special aid for the salvation of the devoted wearer. Traditionally, Mary is said to have appeared before and given the scapular to an early Carmelite monk named Saint Simon Stock."

"The Blessed Virgin Mary?" Peter asked as he stared at the squares now in his hand.

"One and the same," Gavenrael answered.

"I can wear this under the robe, can't I? It doesn't need to be shown to Krampus, or does it?"

"It is for your protection and strength, not to be flayed about like some medal. As long as you know you have it, it will imbue your spirit with power, and Mary's protection. That is all that matters."

"Anything else?" Peter asked.

"That should be more than sufficient for the devil,

himself, let alone Krampus. Besides as I have told you time and again, you are the strongest weapon against him. Your spirit alone should be strong enough to defeat him. I only hope we meet up with him sooner than later."

"Be worried about what you hope for, it may happen," said Peter.

"If you are ready for him, I will be ready with you," Gavenrael replied, "Let's resume our exercises, shall we? We'll pick up at the last position we left off at. Place your left foot firmly a little behind your back..."

Gavenrael stayed with Reverend Goinpeace in a special room in the front of the chapel. She had become quite the mystery, as she never ventured through the North Pole community and was spied by a scant few. Although as in all things, her identity and her purpose were known throughout the North Pole.

Often the good pastor would offer her to dine with him. She politely refused to say that she had everything she needed. He never saw her eat, and she only went on short excursions around the chapel, never venturing far.

Sometimes she was not seen at all for a day or two. Only once Peter returned for more instructions and training would she suddenly show up. Her garb was always the same. The black robe and hood. Often as she was working with Peter's spirit she would place the hood over her head.

She explained to Peter this was so he would not be distracted looking at her. She needed his complete concentration during the cleansing of his spirit. He wondered what she wore under the robe, but was too embarrassed, and a little afraid to learn, to actually dare ask.

Occasionally Peter would find her in the garden praying when he came, but mostly she was always waiting for his arrival in the chapel.

They always started with breathing exercises and then meditation. Once he had meditated, they would begin several physical exercises, which taught him to move more quickly than he ever had before.

"You must be nimble and adroit in the presence of a demon," she said, "If you are too slow they will attack you sensing no strength to evade or hold them off. Always remember the first rule."

Peter responded, "Demons hate to fight for their prey."

"Right." she would answer, "And you must consider yourself as that prey along with anyone else in the room. Do not make the mistake that in trying to protect a child, you, yourself, may be possessed or taken if off guard."

"You have said, his interest in me is little. Was that to not scare me earlier?"

Gavenrael shook her head and said, "I will assume that he will be ordered to not destroy or take you with him. But he may try to possess you and take your spirit to get you out of his way. He will want to make sure his master is served unless he suffers a far worse fate than anything you could remotely imagine."

Sometimes she would act like Krampus, cursing and yelling obscenities to him in a fierce foreign voice. She would make him close his eyes and envision the demon before him. A few times she genuinely frightened him, which she said was good. He could not be properly trained unless he could experience what he might actually meet with in real life. It made him shiver on more than one occasion.

"Never let your guard down. Ever! The moment you do

he will take every advantage to ensnare you. And never listen to his lies. You were not nearly frightened enough when I was yelling those things to you just now."

He protested, "That's because I knew it was you. Though you sounded more like him, I knew it was you."

"Then use that. When you hear his voice again, picture me instead. It may give you an edge over him."

"I don't know if that will work."

She then rose what seemed to be a foot taller and roared in a foul voice that rattled Peter to his very core, "You will obey me or I will take you to Satan, myself!"

Peter raised his arms in terror and defense and cowered before her.

Just as quickly she returned to her normal voice and size and said, "And how about now?"

"Please don't ever do that again," he said meekly.

She smiled and said, "It was just me. You said I didn't scare you."

He said, "Is that how you intend to talk to the demon? Because that sounded more frightening than he did."

"I am not sure what I will do when we meet him. A lot will depend on you. I am only here to assist you, after all."

When December rolled around Peter felt as ready as he ever would be to face the "other Krampus" and told Santa of this fact. Santa was thankful to have Gavenrael's help and told her as much when they met. She assured Santa that she thought Peter would be able to confront this demon on his own, but she was more than willing to lend a hand should the need arise.

So once more they set off in one of the flying machines

for their rendezvous just south of the Spanish coast where the three of them boarded the boat that was waiting. Gavenrael seemed unimpressed with the flying boat, almost as if she knew of the invention beforehand.

Once more they were met by a large crowd. Only now they were yelling for Knecht Ruprecht almost as loudly as St. Nicholas. Many years of their visits had passed and the calendar had advanced to 1902.

As in the past, there was no sign of the demon through most of Europe. Peter had left the switches where he needed. Gavenrael was fascinated watching Peter do his job. Several times before he left the switches he would ask a child if the boy or girl was sorry for the things they had done. If they sounded contrite enough, he would often pull treats from his robe instead of leaving switches.

Gavenrael would tease Peter saying he was too soft-hearted and the switches might have done more good. He would fire back that she had met too many demons in her travels and that children still had the most innocent of hearts if given half a chance.

"Only time may tell. The so-called innocent you spare today, may turn into a genuine hellion tomorrow," she chided.

"I have enough of those to deal with today," he shot back, "And it seems some years there are much more than there used to be."

The travelers entered into Northern Germany and Peter told Gavenrael that this was the start of Krampus' "territory" and that many children had gone missing from here, northward, and they should be on guard.

As they approached one house they heard a great commotion and a woman screaming the name of her daughter. Through the muffled screams they heard someone say,

"Krampus has taken her! Why would he do that?"

They moved away from the house, but now knew they must be close to the demon. As they moved into Austria, Peter felt a great shift in his consciousness near Linz. He went into the house of a 14-year-old boy he had not remembered visiting before. He gazed at the young man and felt a terrible sadness he had never felt before with any child.

What was interesting was that he could not see anything that the boy had done wrong to deserve being imprisoned, but felt he was a pure evil nonetheless. He was vexed on what he should do. He stood at the foot of the youngster's bed and was about to ask Gavenrael when he realized something had changed.

"Get away from my master's child you puny little piece of dung!" Krampus growled at Peter.

Peter stood tall and said, "How have you hidden this evil from my eyes for so long?"

"You are not permitted to even gaze upon this boy. He is destined for greatness as a favored son of Satan. You are to leave and never return to this house or him."

"I think you will be doing the leaving tonight!" Peter turned to the demon and thought of his lovely wife and the joy she brings to every day of Peter's life.

Krampus screamed out loud and told Peter to leave immediately. Peter stood his ground and said, "Not until you have returned every child you have taken, and leave this world never to return!"

The demon screamed loudly and yelled at Peter, "Why you insolent little peasant. Who do you think you are to give me orders! I am commanded by the Prince of all Darkness. It is his bidding that shall be done tonight! I have come prepared for you and you will be sorely sorry you did not heed my last warning!"

The demon began speaking in several foreign languages all at once, and through it Peter heard the monster say, "I have brought many to deal with the likes of you!" And he commanded his legion to take possession of Peter.

What he heard in reply made the demon howl with rage. "You think a little red oil will keep you safe from me? You have no idea who you are dealing with!"

"I know precisely who I deal with – an unclean, unfit servant of a dark world. I am the light from light and I banish you from this earth, but not before I do this."

Peter pulled out the salt and poured it around the room in front of himself and the boy. Krampus stepped back as if he had thrown fire before him. Peter quickly opened a portal and shoved the boy into it. He closed the portal before the Legion could react.

"Here he is and here he will remain until all the children taken have been returned, and you have left this world. Just how important is your master's son?" asked Peter.

The Legion screamed as one and a deafening noise filled the room. They said in unison, "And NOW you have sealed your doom! We were not permitted to destroy you unless you interfered with this boy, but now that you have we can do everything short of killing you until you beg us to let you die just before you release him."

From a dark corner of the room, a black-robed figure stepped out that the demon had not noticed.

"That is not the way this will play out," said the voice in the robe softly.

"Be gone whoever you are!" ordered the demons, "We have complete dominion over this, and we have our master's permission to do as we please!"

Continuing in a calm voice the robe said, "Ah, yes, that is as may be. But you do not have my master's permission, and that is all that matters!"

Suddenly the robe flew off and there stood Gavenrael in a radiant dress of white and gold. Pure light streamed all around her body as she unfurled two immense wings from behind her and drew a golden sword from a belted sheath.

She turned to Peter and said calmly, "You may now use your first vial."

Peter stood staring at her in momentary shock until what she told him finally registered. He pulled the green vial of St. Patrick's holy water and began to pull the stopper out.

"Wait! We must consult with our master!" shrieked the demons.

A moment later the demon in an entirely different voice asked, "What is it you want of me?" It was a terrible guttural voice that shook the floorboards where they stood.

Peter knew in his soul that this was now the voice of Satan, Himself.

He looked at the being and feeling his own positive power said in an unwavering voice, "As you are Satan, I ask for the return of the children that were taken over the past years, and to not take any more unnaturally from this world, as your demon has done. I also request that you are to keep your demons from walking this earth and interfering with me henceforth."

The voice laughed and said, "Do you not understand I could light you up in flames for a thousand years without any effort on my behalf?"

"And that same thousand years the son you have placed here would be in my possession. For I'll not release him unless this is done."

A long pause ensued as if everything had once more been frozen in time. Then the creature finally spoke.

"If I was to do this, you will never interfere with him again. I will move him and you shall not seek him out. And if you find him, he is to be left alone. And that cursed Angel must also agree to this!"

Peter looked at Gavenrael and she nodded saying, "My mission is solely to help you. This is between our God and Satan to sort out. If you would be satisfied, then this bargain shall be made, and I will not interfere further. History will bear this out in the future. You may do as you wish."

"What if his spawn does more damage in the future than if I allow what has already happened with his demon?" Peter asked Gavenrael.

"You cannot control the destiny of all mankind, you may only control what you are allowed to control. There will always be death and horror, just as in the past. You only have oversight over the here and now."

"You are Satan, how do I know the Father of Lies will keep his word?" Peter asked the demon before him.

"You do not, and if you torment me any further, then I may not. I can always create another son. Just consider that you caught me in an affable manner."

Peter said, "Then take your Legion, return the children, and let this be done."

The voice of the Krampus demon returned and said, "You are to forget the name and never seek or discuss, Adolf Hitler with anyone ever again. You will see your punishment for your bargain in your future."

Then the Krampus before him howled mightily and ran through the door writhing in pain.

Peter released his prisoner and was sickened at the

amount of evil that lay before him. Because of the freezing of time and space by both parties, the boy had been undisturbed by all that had taken place around him.

Gavenrael had secured her sword and fastened the robe around herself. She said to Peter, "You have done well, Peter. Never regret your decision. If you had not interfered, all those other children would remain in Hell. And he," she said, pointing at Adolf, "would still be set for his future, however terrible it may be."

"Are you leaving me now?" Peter asked.

"My ordered undertaking is complete. However, I shall leave you one last gift along with the others I have given you."

She bent over and kissed Peter's forehead and whispered, "You will remember all I have taught you and all I have given you, but you will not remember me." She then transported them both, along with Avalanche, with her thought to the town where Santa and Amerigo were just entering and disappeared.

"How are we doing?" asked Santa as they approached each other.

"Everything is returned to normal," answered Peter, "I believe the demon has been completely dispatched from our world and the children returned."

"Truly? You are quite amazing if you accomplished all that! Maybe you should take over my job?"

"No thanks, this one has been quite challenging enough. It will be nice to be cursed for only the things I've done, and not the things I haven't," Peter said with an exhausted smile.

The two moved north toward into Scandinavia and met up with Boutros once more. Peter was quite exhausted from the confrontation with the Satan and Krampus but traveled with his companions letting Boutros do most of the deliveries as in the past.

CHAPTER SEVENTEEN

The battle was a blur in Peter's mind. Most memories were fuzzy, but everyone wanted to know the details. No more so then Cyril Goinpeace, who pressed for every detail.

"I plan to write an ecumenical paper on the subject and need all the details you have. I would like to know how you got all these wonderful items to help vanquish Satan, himself!" Cyril said, clearly excited about the results of Peter first meeting the Krampus demon, and then Satan.

True to his bargain, Peter said nothing about Satan's son, and only referred to an unknown boy in the bed when he arrived. He did say how he moved him to a protected space where he could not be harmed, which was technically true, even if Peter's reason was different.

None of them remembered anything about Gavenrael Devereaux, and if you had mentioned the name blank stares would have resulted.

One thing Cyril told Peter is that he had prayed almost continuously after their first meeting when he learned of the demon. He kept praying to God for help for Peter, knowing Peter was going to take on this demon whether he had His help or not. It was obvious to Cyril that God had answered his prayers.

"No doubt, Reverend," Peter answered when Cyril told him of this fact. He could only shrug his shoulders when asked where the spiritual gifts came from, although Peter could tell you with absolute certainty what each one was, and their use.

Sky would insist that whenever Peter left for his journeys that he wear the brown scapular under his robe. "Wherever it came from, or however you got it, it is a gift from God and will protect you from harm, whether seen or unseen."

Peter agreed and also secretly carried one of the holy water vials, though never the clear one. He would also make certain to anoint himself with red oil before leaving. Finally, for good measure, he put a bag of salt at the base of his bag of switches, just in case.

In 1954, Santa decided it was time to turn the reins over to his son, Nicholas. That same year Knecht Ruprecht announced to both Santas that this was to be his last ride. He said ever since the end of World War II, children were becoming less misbehaved, either that or he was having trouble distinguishing between good and bad anymore.

Santa had witnessed the effects the war in Europe had on Peter and figured this day was coming. He had told Nicholas of his suspicion regarding Peter. Santa had also viewed a marked decrease in the emphasis on Knecht Ruprecht from the towns they had visited during and after the war, Santa thought that this festival had run its course. All the emphasis was on Christmas and Christmas Eve now.

Neither Santa argued with Peter, and both thought that he had earned some quiet around the holidays. Peter and Sky, now married for 165 years, were trying for a family of their own. "Who knows?" Peter said to Nicholas, "Maybe our children will grow up together and carry on our traditions. Then one day you can retire like your father?"

They had a good laugh over this and Nicholas told him that the journey would not be the same without him.

Boutros, now mostly referred to as Zwarte Piet, only traveled with Santa until the 1930's when he seceded from the pair.

Santa told Nicholas that he felt much of the interest and excitement had gone out of their ancestor's holiday. He was saddened by this overall but knew the world was changing rapidly. Some years he would see a revitalization of the holiday and more would celebrate the Feast of St. Nicholas. But other years, hardly at all it seemed.

But in Germany, Austria, Scandinavia and other parts of the Alpine region, the monster Krampus was always bantered about with horrifying stories and threats to children who misbehave. Santa often wondered if they knew just how terrible that creature truly was?

Peter had kept the horrible knowledge about the devil's seed to himself. He never discussed Hitler or his terrible war on the world with anyone, including Sky. Several nights he cried for the world and the horrible evil he had unleashed on it. Making matters worse, some of the children he rescued from the devil were nearly as evil as the devil's seed, himself.

But there were also heroes that came forth. People that had taken their horrible ordeal and made the most of it by helping others and often saving many lives. Life is always a balance scale. Good cannot happen without bad. And evil will always be countered by virtue. The scales may tip back and forth, but one will never completely sway the other for long. That is the way God planned it. No night without day, no desert without the forest, and no Krampus without Peter.

THE END.

About The Author

Joe Moore has written millions of words over his lifetime. A graduate from California State University, Northridge, Joe is a former publisher, editor, advertising, marketing and sales executive. He worked on hundreds of campaigns and articles with thousands of proposals and stories for everything from fishing equipment to business magazines. This may help explain why he is able to write in so many genres.

Moore was a former feature writer for several Southern California periodicals. He has three books published in his Santa Claus Trilogy – *Believe Again, The North Pole Chronicles* and *Faith, Hope & Reindeer* and *Glaciers Melt & Mountains Smoke.* He is very excited to have several children's books also published. *Santa's World Introducing Santa's Elf Series, Jamie Hardrock, Chief Mining Elf, Shelley Wrapitup, Master Design Elf, Keeney Eagleye, Naughty/Nice List Manager, Sarah Buttons, Master Doll Maker* and *Ford MacHarley, Master Wheelsmith* all for Santa's Elf Series©. These books are produced for early readers, written in rhyme, and illustrated by Moore's wife, Mary. Moore has written over a dozen children's stories for the Santa's Elf Series that will be published at the rate of two per year.

Moore has been seen and interviewed on nearly every news program, such as Good Morning America, Fox News, ABC/NBC/CBS News and in numerous radio programs and newspapers. He also appeared on Disney Surfers, Nickelodeon, in numerous parades, on billboards and he and his wife were featured guests on Wealth TV with the late Charlie Jones (NFL Media Hall of Fame announcer). As a professional Santa Claus, he currently is the premiere Santa Claus for Hello Santa digital Santa visits and works with daycare centers, visited dozens of homes and corporations, and spread his goodwill and joy with Mrs. Claus everywhere they travel.

Joe and Mary Moore, (as Santa and Mrs. Claus) also give of themselves, having contributed countless hours (and toys) to worthy charities including, the American Cancer Society, Children's Hospitals, Military families, Domestic abuse shelters, Community projects for schools, "Angel" programs, Hospice centers and more. Both Joe & Mary feel truly blessed by God to be able to bring such joy and happiness to others.

Moore has now written another novel in a third and completely separate genre from his earlier works. He has entered the world of Suspense/Horror with the publishing of *Return of the Birds*. This book picks up 50 years after the birds attacked Bodega Bay in California. Moore's book will have readers on the edge of their seat and searching the skies.

Moore's other passion is cooking! He enjoys creating spectacular meals for Mary and his friends. He also enjoys fishing, even though he admits his wife can always out fish him!

The Moores reside in the beautiful Smoky Mountains of East Tennessee.